GOLDENROD

HERBERT HARKER

Goldenrod

RANDOM HOUSE

New York

Library of Congress Cataloging in Publication Data

Harker, Herbert.
Goldenrod.

I. Title.
PZ4.H282Go3 ⌈PR6058.A686⌉ 813'.5'4 78–37045
ISBN 0–394–47890–8

Manufactured in the United States of America
by Haddon Craftsmen, Scranton, Pennsylvania

2 4 6 8 9 7 5 3

First printing

FOR *Beryl*

GOLDENROD

CHAPTER I

JESSE and his boys had traveled for three days. Now it was evening again, and as he looked back across the distance they had come, Jesse saw their long-legged shadows ripple over the uneven prairie behind them. He was weary beyond feeling. The numbness of his body was intensified by the ache that hung inside him, swinging with the motion of the saddle. Sometimes that ache seemed suspended from his heart and sometimes from his broken pelvis.

"Boys," he said, "we should be there soon."

The pinto Shetland that jogged beside his horse carried his two sons. The one who rode behind was half as old, and looked about half as big, as the one in the saddle. "Are we going to sleep in a bed tonight?" the older boy asked.

"Tonight we sleep in style," Jesse replied. "John Tyler Jones'll probably bed us down on feather mattresses."

The wind had stopped and a hush came over the prairie, as if the going down of the sun were a solemn ordinance. The saddles creaked in cadence, the bridles clinked, the horses' hooves fell in jagged syncopation on the sod. Beneath them lay the river valley, broad and shadowed, with the white skein of water tangled among the trees. An owl swept out of the darkness, directly at them, arced, and with an almost processional beat of wings, faded swiftly into the prairie. To the east, the distant hills still held the light, as a stone remains warm after the fire is out.

As the riders forded the river and came up on the flat, they saw a few buildings set among the trees and the dim outline of a pole corral. A dog barked.

"Shut up, Spider!" a man's voice said. The barking paused, and then began again, moving closer. When they had passed him, the dog fell in behind them, silent now.

The man was standing beside the corral gate. As they stopped in front of him, the big horse lowered its head with a weary snort.

"I'm looking for the Jones ranch," Jesse said. "John Tyler Jones."

The man at the gate replied, "Who do you think you're talking to?"

Jesse urged his horse closer. He leaned forward in his saddle, squinting at the man. "Why, sure, I didn't recognize you there against the light." Jesse got off his horse, and extended his hand to J. T. Jones. "Your directions brought us out right on the nail." He motioned to the boys. "Climb down, fellows. This is the place, all right. J. T., I'd like you to meet my boys." As they came to stand beside him, he said, "This is Ethan. And the little fellow is George."

J. T. Jones said, "What do you mean, this is the place?"

"I mean this is the place we've been traveling three days to reach. I know I told you I'd be here Wednesday, but I had some business to straighten out."

"I ever seen you before?" J. T. Jones asked.

Jesse took off his hat. "It's Jesse Gifford," he said.

"Jesse Gifford?"

"Saturday night," Jesse explained. "In the Alexander Hotel in Lethbridge. You gave me a job bronc-bustin', and I'm here to take it."

[*4*]

"Saturday night?" J. T. Jones repeated.

"You were my long-lost brother on Saturday night. Man, you had just the spot for a man like me. It was shoulder to shoulder, you and me."

"Shoulder to shoulder?" J. T. asked.

"Shoulder to shoulder and bolder and bolder" it had been, sung off key and at the top of their voices.

"Bronc-bustin'," J. T. added, as if the words had been delayed and just reached him. "What would I want with a bronc-buster?"

The song that Jesse was about to sing suddenly died; was killed by J. T.'s words, as cruel as bullets. "You really don't remember?" he said.

"Mister," J. T. said, "I was in Lethbridge on Saturday night. And if I was in Lethbridge, I was drunk. And if I was drunk, who knows what I did?"

"Then you don't have a job at all?"

"I start haying in a week or two. I can use a man then."

"When I bust broncs, that's all I do," Jesse said. "And I get fifty bucks a month."

J. T. laughed. "And when was the last time you busted broncs?"

It had been five years ago—on a windblown camp way out on the Milk River Ridge. "There's not too much call for my kind of work any more," he admitted. "Why else do you think I'd leave a good job wrangling and ride three days to get here?"

"You quit your job?" J. T. exclaimed. "If you take my advice, you'll turn right around and go get it back."

Jesse could hear San Soucie laugh if he ever showed up at the Gillespie gate again. And that pompous Frenchman would probably hire him back, just so he could dig his spurs in Jesse's flanks some more. "You need a man for haying?" Jesse said.

"That's right," J. T. replied. "I'll need a man, but that doesn't start for a week or so."

"Do you have a colt or two you'd like me to work with till then?"

"I can't afford it," J. T. replied. "All the horse-breaking I have to do can be handled after supper."

"It wouldn't cost you anything," Jesse said.

"It would cost me board for the three of you."

"I don't expect you to board us. Isn't there some place hereabouts we could live? All we need is a stove and a roof."

"You claim you rode out here on my say-so," J. T. said, "and maybe you did. I've done some damn-fool things when I was drunk. So you move into the old Hazlett place, and when haying starts, I'll give you a job."

Jesse and the boys ate supper with John Tyler Jones—except that George fell asleep on his chair before he'd taken three bites—and then instead of offering them a feather bed, J. T. directed them to the old Hazlett place, a half a mile down the river. When they got there they found a two-room shack with the door partway open. As they clumped inside, Ethan with the lantern, and Jesse carrying George, they heard mice skitter for the corners. In the second room were two board beds fastened to the walls, and Jesse lay George on one of them. Then, while Ethan tended the horses, Jesse untied the ungainly bedroll from behind his saddle and carried it into the kitchen. There by lantern light he dismembered it—kettles, winter coats, clothing, their few remaining groceries, and a variety of ragged quilts and blankets. Within a few minutes they were lying in bed, Jesse on one side of the narrow room and the boys on the other.

Presently Ethan said, "Do you think Mama will come back, Jesse?"

"No. I don't think so."

"It was sure fun to live with her, wasn't it? I mean, when we were all together?"

"It sure was."

"Remember that time she gave San Soucie the piece of chocolate pie?"

"Go to sleep," Jesse said.

"I'll never forget the look on old San Soucie's face."

"Yeh," Jesse agreed. "That was funny, wasn't it?"

"Jesus Christ, I miss her."

"She wouldn't want you talking that way."

"Then why doesn't she come home and stop me?"

"She's not coming home."

"She might. You don't know what she's going to do, Jesse."

That had been proved well enough. "No. I don't."

"So. She might come back."

Jesse lay with his hands clasped behind his head. He turned to look across the room where his sons lay. The rough patterns of the night were gray on gray. "Goodnight, Ethan," he said.

The boy did not reply—perhaps he was asleep already. Jesse sighed against the gray and breathing world in which he lived. Somewhere beyond that world he saw his wife. He raised his arm across his eyes and turned his face to the wall. It had been years now—two years—since he had seen her, and still the hollow of his body felt as tender as a wound where some part has been torn away. "Oh, God," he breathed. He himself could not have said if it was a curse or a prayer.

CHAPTER II

THE next day Jesse was awake shortly after daylight. He did not get up at once, but lay looking at the spot the sun made on the whitewashed wall above the boys' bed. The interior of the house was not bad—heavy cobwebs and dust of course, but saved from the gloominess of most settlers' shacks by the skim of whitewash that someone had brushed on it, perhaps years before. It was home now, anyway—for how long, he could not even guess.

He had been at Gillespie's for four years. Each day for four years he had felt a small diminishment, a lowering, as if another drop of vital force had seeped away. And he had seen clearly the husk that would be left after the force was gone. He had not seen it in his imagination, nor in a dream, but in the person of an actual man—Lars, the chore boy at Gillespie's, sixty, dry and bent as an old peapod, gray-colored, muttering: Lars now, but in ten years his name would be Jesse. That's the way San Soucie saw Jesse—as the raw material for another Lars, younger and longer-wearing. And every day he had worked at it, shaping Jesse, bending him, draining him, setting him to dry, scooping out his guts, till all he'd have left would be a shell, cheap to feed, easy to manage, with just enough weight to lift a broom or a pitchfork, and enough strength to clean the stable.

He couldn't have survived at Gillespie's. Even now he wondered if he had gotten away in time. He felt a great weariness in every limb, and his life seemed distant and flickering, as though San Soucie or his wife, Shirley, had set

it down beyond his reach. But he wasn't old yet. All he
needed was a little rest, a chance to get his head up, and
he'd be all right. Perhaps J. T.'s was the place he'd been
looking for.

He left the boys asleep, saddled his horse, and headed
up the hill toward Lone Rock, his hat slanted over his eyes,
his roll of money in his pocket. Besides the need for some
groceries, he felt a hankering for adult companionship. In
his heyday he had more friends than he could count—cowboys, ranchers, bankers, newspapermen. Then had come
the ride on Sundown—the ride that would clinch the championship for him; the ride and the lost stirrup, and Sundown's hoof in the small of his back, and for months afterward nothing but misery and the slow erosion of people he
called friends.

As he topped the hill and saw the prim green town with
its grain elevators standing over it, he knew that the sort of
companionship he was after could not be found in Lone
Rock. He didn't fancy a day spent with the village derelicts
in the cool garage, tossing nickels at a line on the floor.

When he got to town, the store was not yet open. For
the better part of an hour he hunkered on the step, or
walked up and down the board sidewalk, while the cool air
of early morning was slowly dispersed by the wind from the
mountains. By the time the store opened, three other men
and a woman were also waiting. They greeted each other as
they met, and the men talked while the woman stood pa-
tiently, looking down the street. None of them paid any
attention to Jesse.

Finally a tall humped man unlocked the door from the
inside, then walked behind the counter to face his custom-
ers. He was joined by a pretty girl, perhaps sixteen or so,
who turned to Jesse and asked, "Can I help you?" He

bought flour, sugar, coffee, bologna, potatoes, canned vegetables, pork and beans, butter, bacon, evaporated milk, eggs, strawberry jam. He got a loaf of bread as a treat for the boys, and some tailor-made cigarettes for himself.

For some reason Jesse always felt good when he was spending money. He'd managed to save almost two hundred dollars while he was at Gillespie's, but a bank account never gave him any satisfaction. Only now, as he peeled a ten-dollar bill off the roll in his pocket, put it on the counter, pocketed his change, and took his purchases, did money seem to have any relation to his life. It seemed then, in the act of parting with it, to purify him somehow, as if along with the money he was sloughing off unhappy memories and fears for the future.

He whistled as he rode his horse back out of town. The warm wind blew out of the mountains behind him and seemed to push him along, so that almost before he knew it he was headed down the river hill toward his home. The shack was long and narrow, with a low-pitched roof which gave it an appearance of friendly shelter. Chop out the jungle of weeds and thistles which surrounded it, put in a couple of lilac bushes, give it a coat of paint and a little furniture, and it would make a home good enough for any man.

J. T. Jones' car was stopped in the lane in front of the house. He had not expected to see J. T. again until haying started. At the gate, he got off Czar, took down his box of groceries from the back of the saddle, and started toward the house. George came running down the path toward him. "Did you get some bologna?" he asked.

"Yes. I got you some bologna."

"J. T. Jones is here."

"I saw his car."

[*10*]

"Can we have breakfast now?"

"Yes sir. Right now. I'm hungry as a bear."

"*Rowr!* Me too," George said.

As Jesse walked into the house he could see that Ethan and J. T. Jones were sitting across from each other on the beds in the back room. "Howdy, J. T.," he said. He put the grocery box on the table.

J. T. came and stood in the doorway. "Hello, Jesse," he said.

"Have you had breakfast?"

"Long ago," J. T. replied. "Did you ever run a tractor?"

Jesse loathed tractors. He never knew what to expect from them, or what to do if they stopped. They were noisy and smelly. "Sure," he said. "Gillespie's had three tractors. I used to run one every so often." He set the frying pan and the coffeepot on the front of the stove, and looked in his box for the bacon, eggs, bologna, and coffee.

"I've got some summerfallow needs working," J. T. went on. "Probably take about three days. I'll pay you two dollars a day, seven till seven."

"You want me to start this morning?" Jesse asked.

"No," J. T. replied. "My cultivator's broke. I've got to go to Macleod tomorrow and get it welded. You can start the next day—no, that's Sunday. Start Monday morning."

"I'll be there," Jesse said. "How's chances to go to town with you tomorrow?"

"To Macleod?"

"There's a few things I need."

"Sure. I'll pick you up."

George had been unloading the grocery box. "Oh boy," he cried. "Baker's bread."

The bacon and eggs were frying now, all scrambled

[*11*]

together in the frying pan. J. T. walked through the kitchen toward the door. "See you tomorrow," he said.

"This coffee's about ready," Jesse said. "Might as well stop and have a cup."

J. T. paused. "Maybe I will," he said. "That bacon sure smells good, too."

"There's plenty," Jesse said. "Get some plates down, Ethan. We'll have to go in the bedroom to sit down, though. There isn't room in here for all of us." He scooped the eggs onto one tin plate, then returned the pan to the stove and put four slices of bread to toast in the bacon grease. Within a few moments the four of them were sitting on the beds, tin plates of hot food in their hands and cups of coffee on the floor at their feet.

"Tastes good," J. T. said. "The truth is, I didn't eat much breakfast. It was too early in the morning." J. T. sat chewing, and looked around the room.

Jesse, also chewing, followed his gaze. He wouldn't get high marks for housekeeping, but J. T. wasn't paying him for that, anyway. Heavy cobwebs still clustered in the ceiling corners. The soft flannelet undersides of the beds were exposed beneath a misshapen sworl of covers. Clumps of overalls and jackets hung from nails on the wall. "We haven't cleaned house yet," Jesse said. "That's the first thing on the docket this morning."

"It's hard for a man alone," J. T. agreed. "Nine years since I buried the missus. It's been hard."

Between the beds was a low wooden table which held a tin of tobacco, a red bandana, a hunting knife, the stump of a pencil, a bullet lighter, a spool of thread, some horseshoe nails, an old police whistle, and a Bible. In the midst of it all stood a small oval picture frame, like an arch among ruins. It was a photograph of Shirley. Her face

looked up out of the picture, her eyes deeply shadowed by
lashes, her hair falling across her cheek.

"She looks pretty young," J. T. Jones said at last.

"She was when that was taken," Jesse said.

"What did she die of?"

"She isn't dead."

After a minute Ethan said, "She ran off with another
man."

J. T.'s eyes darted to meet Jesse's, and then away again.
"Oh," he said.

Jesse knew what he was thinking, something like: My
wife died. The Lord took her. I couldn't help that, could I?
But let some mortal man fool around with her, and he
would have been dead. And she with him. It was the way
they all thought—the hands at Gillespie's, the boys in town,
the barber, the feed man, the waiter in the beer parlor:
What kind of man are you? Married men, single men,
drunkards, chasers, cattle thieves—they'd all known him
and Shirley. They said something like, "Gee, Jesse. That's
tough." But what they thought was: You poor son-of-a-
bitch. Whatever made you think you could hold a woman
like her?

J. T. wiped his plate with a piece of toast and put it in
his mouth. Then he drank the rest of his coffee. "Thanks,"
he said.

"Come again," Jesse said.

J. T. set his cup carefully in the middle of his tin plate,
as though it were the least he could do to bring order into
the world. He spoke with calm deliberation. "I always
figured a man can make his choice between a beautiful
woman and a faithful one." He stood, holding the cup
firmly in place, checking it with his eye to be sure it was the
same distance from the edge of the plate on every side.

"Mine were faithful," he said. "Both of 'em." He walked out through the kitchen. The plate clattered on the table as the outside door closed, and then squeaked open again. They heard his car door slam, heard the car start, and saw it drive by the window, back up the hill.

"Let's go hunting," Ethan said. "See if we can get some meat for dinner."

"Maybe after a while," Jesse said. "You fellows go outside and play. I want to clean up the house a little." He knew he should make the boys help, but it would be easier to do it himself.

Jesse sat on the bed, alone. I'd have killed 'em both, if it was me. I'd have followed 'em to Greenland if I had to, and killed 'em in their tracks. That was what they all thought, but what did they know about it? That's the first thing Jesse had thought, too. He had taken his hunting knife and gone after them—the shotgun was too awkward to carry and seemed too impersonal. He wanted to look them in the eye while he stabbed them—flesh on flesh. He wanted to hear them scream and feel their blood grow cool as it dried on the back of his hand.

There'd been no warning, or at least he didn't read the signs. He came home after work one night and found the fire out in the kitchen stove, and the boys playing alone in the dusk of the living room. The house held an emptiness as heavy as death. He knew she'd gone. He lit the lamp and went to the old wardrobe where she kept her dresses and her high-heeled shoes. The dresses were all there, and the shoes, more worn than he remembered, were lying at curious angles on the floor of the wardrobe. In the bureau drawer he found the slacks she wore around the house and her underthings. Her other pair of shoes lay abandoned on the floor by the bed. She must have been naked when she left the house.

Ethan and George, younger then, were standing behind him. "I'm hungry," Ethan said. "Where's Mama?"
"Didn't you see her?" Jesse asked. "Did she tell you
where she was going?"
"She just told us to go down and play in the gully. And
when we came back she was gone."
"You didn't see anybody?"
"Uh-uh. We just came back, and she was gone."
She didn't leave a note. He looked for one, offhandedly
at first, as if it didn't matter, then more earnestly. Before the
night was out he had searched in every crevice of the house
that was large enough to hold a slip of paper. And all night,
as he searched, he seemed to remember little remarks she'd
made that might have warned him if he had listened.
Before the sun was up he woke Ethan, and told him to
stay out of school and look after George until he got back.
And he'd gone after them, the scabbard strapped to his belt
and his hand touching the knife. For a while he tried to
pretend that she had gone alone, that she had only wanted
to get away for a day or two. But she couldn't have gone
alone. Somebody had to bring her some clothes—a new
dress, and new shoes, and black silk stockings . . . He knew
the kind of clothes a man like that would bring.
It took him all day on the train to get to Calgary. And
when, wandering the city streets in the early morning, he
came across Keno's McLaughlin Buick parked in front of
the Empress Hotel, he knew he'd found them. The bile
came up in his throat. It was Keno all right.
The finish of the Buick gleamed like a cherry skin. Its
chrome wire wheels caught the sun in a thousand places,
causing the light to dance as if the wheels were still spin-
ning. The car was empty, its heavy glass windows rolled up
tight, enclosing a plush wine vault where misty scents and
echoes of Shirley were sealed away from him. Still, for all

its massive guardianship, and though he tried not to listen, her familiar little sobs and murmurs seemed to reach him.

Bile. Bile in his throat and in his eyes. Choked and blinded by it. Up the hotel steps and in through the big glass doors. The sleepy-looking clerk. The room number. The clerk awake now. The room number. Three fifty-one. The stairs, two at a time. The long hall. The doors, like mileposts. Three hundred and forty-nine miles. Three hundred and fifty miles. Three hundred and fifty-one miles. The feel of the knife on his hip, and its handle in his hand like a healing balm that could cure the poison that filled him. The quiet tap on the door. Keno's voice. The tap again. Waiting. The hard handle of the knife in his palm, but the blade still in its sheath. The boots crossing the floor. Boots! Boots at eight in the morning? Did he sleep in his boots? Keno's voice again, not toward the door now; near the door, but turned back into the room, softly. The door open, just a crack. Keno's eye, under Keno's hat. The door swinging wide. Keno naked to the waist, his skin as white as a root beneath his brown neck and above his wrists. Keno's chest, heavy and molded, matted with curly black hair. Keno's striped trousers and shiny black boots. Keno standing there in his hat and trousers and boots, a polish cloth in his hand.

"Well," Keno said. "We sure didn't expect to see you." He turned back into the room. Keno's shoulders, broad and white, curving inward, down into the sleek striped trousers. "Look who's here."

He followed Keno into the room. Shirley was lying in bed, her shoulders bare. She turned her face away, and slipped deeper under the covers. Keno put his right boot on a chair and snapped the polish cloth across the toe, back and forth, back and forth. "What brings you to town?"

Jesse could see the muscles moving along the arched

back as Keno snapped the cloth. He wondered just where on the broad white rippling back the knife blade should enter to strike the heart. He knew he should act quickly while Keno was still bent over his boots. But he glanced toward Shirley.

"Get out of here," she said, and pulled the blankets over her head. He'd know where her heart was; even under the covers, he'd be able to find it. But as he stood looking at the bed his anger all drained out through the soles of his feet.

Keno gave a final snap with his cloth, and stood up with his shiny black boots planted a foot or so apart. Jesse didn't look at his face again. He knew exactly the expression it wore. In the first glance he had memorized it. He would never forget that face, the face of the champ.

If only things had been different. If he'd been a little earlier. If he'd caught them in bed, naked, defenseless, guilty—how different things might have been. He could have carved them then with pleasure, and God Himself would not have blamed him for it. And he wouldn't have to lie awake now, listening to the moans and sobs that reached him from wherever they happened to be—even from half-way around the world, when Keno went on tour to Australia; moans and sobs and fingernails in his shoulders; Keno's shoulders, broad and white tapering into sleek striped trousers.

A tin plate slid off one of the beds where George had left it, and clattered to the floor. Jesse looked around him, at the dirty dishes, and the unmade beds, and the cobwebs hanging on the walls. Slowly he stacked the dishes and went with them into the kitchen.

CHAPTER III

THAT afternoon, when Jesse had finished sweeping the house and had a rest, he untied one of the shirt bundles that lay in a corner of the kitchen. Among the articles it held were three shotgun shells. "How about some fresh meat for supper?" he said.

George came running. "You bet!"

With the shotgun in his hand, Jesse walked down the path through a forest of sunflowers to the log stable that stood against the fence. The house was obviously makeshift, a homesteader's shack where the family might live until they had the money and leisure to build the kind of house the wife wanted. But the stable, even now, showed evidence of careful workmanship, as if in its carefully fitted logs the builder had tried to carve a symbol that would lend of its perfection to all his efforts—his flocks and his lands and his home. The walls still stood as straight and firm as the day they were laid, but the door was gone from its hinges, and in the front, two square holes stood black and empty, with slivers of glass strewn on the ledge beneath them. The roof had never been finished, so the loft was open to the sky. Only the log that formed the roof beam had been placed, supported by the gables at either end.

Jesse looked around him. The homestead rested between the river and the hill, screened by a cottonwood grove from a view of the water, but still permeated by the gentle sound of it. Far up the valley he could see the pale-blue tops of the mountains, so nearly indistinguishable

[*18*]

from the sky that their form was most clearly defined by a few remnants of snow.

George had come along behind, running silently on bare feet. He took the bridle from a nail on the outside wall of the stable. "I'll catch old Czar," he said. Beneath the cottonwoods on the other side of the pasture, the two horses grazed. George ran through the grass toward them, dragging the bridle behind him.

"Come back here," Jesse said.

George stopped. "I can catch him."

"I don't want him caught."

"Aren't you going hunting?"

"Not on horseback, I'm not." Just the thought of getting into the saddle seemed to start his back hurting all over again. Ethan came around the corner of the stable.

"We're going hunting," George said.

"Hunting for what?" Ethan asked.

"What strikes your fancy?" Jesse said. "Roast duck, partridge pie, or rabbit stew?"

"Roast duck!" George cried.

"It's not duck season," Ethan said.

"All the better," Jesse said. "They won't be expecting us to take a shot at 'em." They all started toward the river. Above the gravel bar, they stopped to skip rocks on a quiet pool. Then they began to hunt more seriously. A few feet apart they walked through the trees and bushes, parallel to the river. "Shh," Jesse cautioned them. "Quiet."

"Here," George cried, and clapped his hand over his mouth. Then he whispered, loudly, "Quick, Jesse. Here. Quick."

But when Jesse got there, he could see nothing. "What is it?"

George was still pointing. "A rabbit. He went right in there. Right in those bushes."

The three of them were side by side now. "Oh, it wasn't, either," Ethan said.

"It was. I saw it."

"Shh," Jesse said. "Now you fellows stay behind me."

He moved forward, bending low between the bushes, shotgun firmly in both hands, ready. There was a flurry in the grass to his right. As he turned, a bush rabbit came into sight, hopped a short distance, and stopped, head high, ears alert. Jesse raised his shotgun and squeezed the trigger. The expected blast of sound and shock against his shoulder did not occur. Nothing. The rabbit still sat there. The quiet of the morning was unbroken.

"Shoot him," Ethan hissed. "Why don't you shoot him?"

Jesse lowered his gun. "Shh," he said. He had forgotten to load. "He's not very big. Maybe he'll lead us to another one."

"Shoot him," Ethan cried, and at the sharp sound of his voice, the rabbit darted away, out of their sight. "Why didn't you shoot him?"

But George was tugging on Jesse's sleeve, pulling him back the way they had just come. His finger was tight against his lips. As they crept back into the coolness of the bushes, Jesse looked where George pointed. At first all he could see was the brown, tangled grass and dead branches that lay on the ground. But then in the midst of it, he saw an eye, and from that beginning he was able to fill in the crouched body of a baby rabbit, its ears pressed flat against its furry back —absolutely motionless.

"Please don't shoot him," George whispered.

"He's not big enough to do any good, anyway," Jesse replied. "Nothing but bones and fur."

"Can I take him home?" George said.

"He'd just die."

"He's so cute. I wish I could take him home. I'd make a pen for him."

"He'd die," Ethan agreed. "I've tried it, George. I've caught baby rabbits lots of times. I've put them in boxes with straw and stuff, and all kinds of food, and milk, and everything. But they won't eat. They just die."

"He's all alone," George said. "He'll die if we leave him here, won't he?"

"That was his mother that hopped away," Jesse said. "She'll come back as quick as we're gone."

George crouched, staring at the tiny creature. Its fur was so soft that it seemed to riffle even in the motionless air beneath the bush. But its eyes did not move, nor any part of its body. George bent over it. "Poor little fella," he said, and reached with his hand, closer and closer, repeatedly stopping and drawing back, then moving it yet closer. At last he touched the rabbit and began to stroke its ears and the soft fur of its back. "See. He's not afraid of me. He likes me."

"Can you feel his heart beating?" Jesse asked.

"Yeh. It's going so fast!"

"That's 'cause he's so scared. Come on now, let's leave him alone."

They started away, but George stopped to look back. "Can I wait until his mother comes? To guard him, so something doesn't happen to him?"

"She won't come as long as we're here," Ethan said.

Reluctantly George turned, and the three of them continued their tramp along the river. As they walked, Jesse loaded his gun.

They were out of the trees, walking beneath the hill, when a flock of partridge flew up almost at their feet. The sudden trill and whir of wings startled the hunters, but almost as a reflex Jesse brought up his gun, aimed, arced the muzzle, and fired. The roar of his second shot echoed against the first. One of the birds, then another, dropped out of formation and fell to the ground. The boys found them in the grass, still fluttering, and Jesse wrung their necks. "Well, boys," he said. "Roast partridge for supper. How does that sound?" They set off toward the house.

As Jesse walked around a clump of purple birch, he found himself face to face with a bally-faced cow. She stood there among the shadows, her tail switching intermittently, her face bland, her eyes on Jesse.

"I bet I can ride her," Ethan said.

"Ride her?"

"Sure. I've got to get practiced up for the stampede, haven't I?"

The idea took Jesse by surprise. Years ago he and Ethan had talked of little except the stampede, but for a long time now they hadn't mentioned it. Jesse said, "You're too young, anyway."

"Not any more, I'm not. This year I'm twelve."

Jesse felt that this was a time for special wisdom. He had raised his son to be a cowboy, but now he wasn't sure. Perhaps the best way was to meet the problem head-on. "I tell you what," Jesse said. "If you can ride that old blister, I'll let you enter the stampede."

"Really?" Ethan said.

Jesse cautioned, "But if she throws you, we all stay home and put up hay for J. T. Jones."

The raised voices caused the cow to lower her head and move to one side. "All right," Ethan said. "As long as I get a surry-single, I'll ride that rooster till the sun goes down."

"Go and get your surry-single, then." Ethan started off

on a run, back toward the house. "Bring the lariat, too," Jesse called after him. He put his partridges down on the grass and sat beside them with his back against a tree.

George came and sat near him.

"Aren't we going to eat?"

"After the stampede," Jesse said. "Ethan's going to put on a stampede for us."

Ethan came back with the coiled lariat over his shoulder and a soft halter rope in his hand. He had stopped at the house long enough to put on his spurs and some fringed leather gauntlets. He walked up and looked around. By now several cattle had drifted close, surrounding them with the sounds of crunching grass and snapping twigs. "Where is she?" Ethan asked.

"Over behind that tree," Jesse said. "Waiting for you with blood in her eye."

Ethan dropped the halter rope beside Jesse, and as he walked toward the cow he shook out his lariat loop.

George jumped up. "I'll go help him."

"You better stay right here," Jesse said. "There's going to be an earthquake over there in a minute."

The cow looked at Ethan suspiciously. Then she swung away, and the boy threw the rope in one swift motion. As the cow plunged to escape she ran right into the loop, pulling the rope tight and yanking Ethan almost out of his boots. Running, he swung as wide as he could around a tree. He didn't get far enough. The rope whirred around the tree trunk, pulling the boy back in a straight course behind the running cow. He tried to dig in his heels, but he had job enough just keeping his feet under him. The brush with the tree had cost him so much rope that he was getting dangerously close to the end of it.

Jesse rose and ambled after his son. "Why don't you

help him?" George cried, running breathlessly along, a little in front of Jesse.

"He wants to be a cowboy," Jesse said.

The trotting cow changed direction just enough to give Ethan a little slack. He raced to one side again, around another tree, playing out what rope he had left as he went. This time he got far enough, and the direction of the cow was such that when the rope came taut it made a deep V, with Ethan at one end, the cow at the other, and the tree in the middle. Both cow and boy were brought up short, and in the instant that followed, Ethan plunged headlong around the tree, clinging to his rope by only the knot in the end of it. Before the cow renewed her rush to get away, the rope had the bite of a full turn around the rough tree trunk, and Ethan was able to pause and improve his hold. The cow hung back at the other end of the rope, muzzle slavered and eyes rolling.

Jesse and George walked up to Ethan. "Well," Jesse said, "now you've got her, what you going to do with her?"

Ethan was puffing. "I'm going to ride her," he said.

"You sure picked a dandy," Jesse said.

Working together, while George drove the cow closer with a stick, Jesse and Ethan pulled in the rope. Soon they had the cow with her jaw neatly fitted around the trunk of the tree. While Ethan held her, Jesse tied the surry-single around her body, a short way behind the front legs.

"If she doesn't buck, the deal's off."

"She'll buck," Ethan said. "I'll spur her till she does."

Now Jesse held the lariat and Ethan walked quietly to the side of the cow. Surry-single in his left hand, he stood back, stepped and jumped, swinging his right leg high, and landed on her back, sitting just behind her shoulders. He clasped the rope firmly with both hands, knuckles down. "Let 'er buck," he said.

Jesse looked over his shoulder. "George. You stand behind that tree. There's no way of telling which direction this show is going to go."

The cow was becoming more and more uneasy. Jesse loosened the rope from the tree and then from the cow's neck, and snatched the loop over her horns. It was done so fast that for a moment the animal didn't know what had happened. Then Ethan's spurs landed in her ribs, and he cried, "Hee—yi!"

The cow's first jump was a reflex, but then, finding herself free from the rope, the spurs still in her ribs, she lowered her head and plunged upward. Jesse had a glimpse of Ethan's face, both frightened and bemused—then it was yanked away with a violence that seemed to deform and darken it. Up, across, and down the face went, off the hat flew, and the boy's dark hair flipped back and forth. The cow bucked in an irregular circle, her head toward the center. With every jump she threw her hindquarters high, at the same time twisting them first to one side and then the other. Occasionally in the progress of the circle, Jesse could see Ethan's face, blurred as it plunged up and down and arced from side to side, but instantaneously in focus each time it changed direction. The boy's body flowed with the movement of the cow, as though his legs were fused so close to her sides that he could feel through the hide each signal of her intention.

Jesse felt a peculiar blending of exultance and dismay inside him. He remembered the thrill—so old that he had almost forgotten it—of his own first ride on a full-grown steer. That thrill had been the initial infection. The disease which followed brought alternating attacks of gaiety and despair so profound that he would not wish it on anybody, least of all his own son. But he could feel the cow's muscles surge as if it were his own legs that clutched them, and he knew that already it was too late to alter the direction which Ethan had taken.

Jesse and George had followed the cow through the trees. At last Jesse shouted, "Okay! Okay!" Ethan closed his legs above the cow's shoulders and jumped clear, jerking the knot so that the rope would loosen and drop off. He landed on his feet, but the thrust of the cow's lunge was too great, and he pitched to the ground, rolling to be sure he was clear of her.

George ran to his brother. Jesse walked over to pick up the halter rope where it had slipped to the ground. The cow stood a short distance away, looking back at him with her head held slightly high. "Well!" Ethan cried. "I guess we go to the stampede, eh?"

"I guess we do," Jesse agreed.

"I can enter the boys' steer-riding?"

"I reckon you can."

"Why don't you enter again, Jesse?"

"Me?" Jesse laughed. "I'm too old for that stuff."

George pulled at his hand. "Now I'm hungry."

"Well, let's go eat then."

They walked back toward the tree with the shotgun leaning against it. As they came near, Jesse noticed something moving in the grass. It was a weasel, its tail up, its long sleek body humped as it tore at the flesh of one of their partridges. Jesse shouted and ran toward it, waving his arms. Even after the weasel looked up and saw him, it could not resist one more bite before it turned and darted away, tiny feathers clinging to its throat. Jesse seized the shotgun and fired. The blast lifted the running weasel off the ground and blew it through the grass. A trailing leg ticked the ground and its body flipped and rolled over, its breast dark with partridge blood and its back splashed with its own.

[26]

The partridge was ruined—open right to the breast-bone. Though the other had not been touched, it was saturated with the weasel odor. Nobody but a weasel could eat it now. Jesse swore. "And I used my last shell to shoot that lousy weasel."

"What are we going to have for supper now?" George asked.

"You start crying, you won't get anything for supper," Jesse told him. As they walked back toward the house he noticed a flock of pigeons perched on the bare roof beam of the stable. A squab pie sounded good now, but as they approached the pigeons flew, circled high and returned to their perches with a loud flutter of wings, unmolested.

They ate canned pork and beans that night, Jesse choking over the thought of the shells he'd forgotten to buy.

CHAPTER IV

WHEN J. T. called at the shack on Saturday morning, Jesse was ready to go. He got into the car and pulled the door; it closed with a solid *chunk*. This was a new Dodge, still with the factory smell about it. Jesse breathed deeply and looked around him. The weight of all the car's elegance was centered in the pebbly fawn-colored dashboard, with its battery of knobs and one large disc of faintly amber glass which held the instruments. Beyond the windshield the long pearly hood was topped with a charging ram. The car moved away as if pulled by a silent, invisible hand.

"I reckon a Dodge is the pick," Jesse said. "I saw this hell-driver's show in Lethbridge last year. Darndest thing I ever did see—bouncing those cars off ramps and off one another, and rolling 'em over till you'd have sworn they'd never turn another wheel. And they just set 'em on their feet again, and away they go, front ends stove in, radiators steaming, fenders flapping, and still they run like crazy." J. T. didn't speak. Jesse looked down at his boots, as gray as dirt against the shiny rubber floor mat. The toes were worn through completely, and from each hole sprouted a little tuft of fuzzy lining. He glanced at J. T. again. Driving the car, the little man thrust his head so far forward that it seemed in danger of pulling loose and rolling down into his lap. His eyes barely cleared the rim of the steering wheel. He didn't look at Jesse and he didn't speak. For all a person could tell, he was alone, driving to town in his shiny new Dodge.

As they drove up in front of the Queen's Hotel in Macleod, Jesse said, "Let me buy you a beer."

J. T. looked at him. "If you got any money, you spend it on somethin' for your kids," he said.

"Listen," Jesse said. "I've got some money, and I'm no freeloader. You give me a trip to town, I buy you a beer. Anything wrong with that?"

"I guess not," J. T. said, and he went with Jesse into the beer parlor. His acceptance was only a formality, though. As they waited to be served, J. T. looked slightly off to one side, as if he were having his picture taken.

"Any idea what time you'll be going home?" Jesse asked.

"An hour or so," J. T. replied. "As soon as I get this extree welded. I'll leave the car where it is." He added, "I can't wait, though."

As soon as his beer came, he drank it and pushed back his chair. For the first time he looked at Jesse. He looked at him deliberately, his eyes traveling slowly from feature to

[*28*]

feature and part to part, as though Jesse were some kind of exhibit. They seemed to linger on the tufted end of the boots. Then they traveled up his body. He still didn't look Jesse in the eye, though. At the last minute his glance veered off toward the clock on the wall. Then as if the sight of the clock were the switch that set him in motion, he rose and left the beer parlor.

Jesse ordered another beer. It looked like today he would be needing all he could get.

The noise of the beer parlor had started to diffuse slightly, and objects across the room began to blur, when he found himself looking again at the figure of J. T. Jones.

"Stand up," J. T. Jones said. Jesse stood up. J. T. bent over and looked at the middle of his stomach. "Where'd you get that?"

"It came with me, as far as I know," Jesse said. "It's filled out a little . . ." He couldn't figure out what J. T. was talking about.

"The belt buckle, you ass," J. T. said. "Where'd you get the belt buckle?"

Jesse liked his belt. It was the only decent piece of clothing he owned—hand-tooled leather two and a half inches wide, with a silver-mounted buckle as big as a postcard. The buckle was embossed with the head of a longhorn steer, and engraved to Jesse Gifford, Saddle Bronc Champ.

J. T. was still bent over, studying the buckle. "How come I never seen it before?"

"I don't wear it every day," Jesse explained. "It's what you might call my Sunday suit."

J. T. straightened up and looked Jesse in the eye. "Well, I'll be damned," he said. "You're Jesse Gifford."

"I told you I was, the first time I saw you."

"I knew I'd heard the name," J. T. said, "but I couldn't place it. It's been a while, you know."

"Yes it has."

"I was on the board of the Southern Alberta Coop the year they gave that trophy. I helped pick it out. Well, I'll be damned." He sat down and filled his glass from Jesse's bottle. He emptied the glass and looked at Jesse again. "I got out there running around town—dropping off my ex-tree at the blacksmith shop, gettin' some new mower guards at IHC, and all the time I knew there was something about you I'd missed. And then it came to me. It was the belt buckle. I'd recognized it, you see, but it didn't register at first. Well, then I wondered where you got it from—if you stole it or something. I still didn't have you connected up, you see." J. T. waved his arm and signaled to the waiter.

Jesse didn't know what to say.

"So you're Jesse Gifford," J. T. said.

"Yes I am."

"Well, I'll be damned." After he'd had a couple of drinks, J. T. seemed better able to collect his thoughts. "How come you quit riding?" he said.

"I broke my pelvis," Jesse said.

"Well, I'll be damned. Didn't it get better?"

"Not really."

After a while J. T. said, "There's money in that game."

Jesse nodded.

J. T. turned his glass around and around between his fingers, while his eyes held steady, looking down into it. "Did you ever think of going back to it?"

"Sure."

"Well. Why don't you?"

It was a fair question. Jesse couldn't answer it, even to

himself. In his day he had broken bones all over his body —arms, legs, fingers, toes, ribs, ankles—even his jaw. But he had always managed to come back and ride again. The pelvis had been different. For some reason it didn't knit properly, and by the time he was able to walk again he'd lost thirty pounds. He had gained the weight back, and more, but his spirit never seemed to recover. "It's hard, with the boys," he explained to J. T. "I can't leave them and I can't take them with me. And it keeps me scratching just to put food on the table. If I hold down a job, I can't go stampeding."

"I got an idee," J. T. said after another pause. "Let's you and me be partners."

"Partners?"

"Yep." J. T. began to speak more quickly. "I'll pay you wages, starting today. Good wages. Thirty dollars a month. When there's a stampede on, we'll go stampedin'. When there ain't, you work for me."

"You mean me go back to riding?"

"Sure. I'll pay the entry fees."

Jesse tried not to get excited. He must remember that this was John Tyler Jones talking—the same man who gave him a job as bronc-buster. This new proposition would probably be forgotten as easily as the other one was. "You don't have to worry about the boys," J. T. went on. "We'll make arrangements to take care of them." The boys could take care of themselves. That was no problem. "By the end of the summer you'll have a sockful of money."

A sort of chill began in Jesse's legs, and moved slowly up his body.

"What do you say?" J. T. asked him, his head teetering on the edge of his shoulders, closer to rolling off than ever before.

[*31*]

Jesse asked, "Are you drunk?"

"Could I be drunk on two bottles of beer?"

"I don't know."

"You're worried about that thing in Lethbridge," J. T. said.

"We were blood brothers that night," Jesse said. "That's even closer than partners."

"I was drunk then. Right now I'm sober as a prophet, and I'll sign my name in blood to every word I say."

"You haven't said anything yet," Jesse told him.

"What did I leave out?"

"What's in it for you?"

"Why, we'd be partners, that's all. I put up the money and you put up the know-how, and we split the winnings."

"Fifty-fifty?"

"Of course, we might never make a dime. But I'm willing to do it, as a sort of favor, you see."

"Don't do me any favors," Jesse said. "I'll give you twenty-five percent."

J. T. snorted. "You'll give me! You won't give me a thing—'cause you haven't a thing to give. You're stranded, mister."

J. T. was right. He didn't have to negotiate. He had his thousand acres and his cattle and his new Dodge, and if he went home that night and never saw Jesse again, he wouldn't be hurt. Jesse wasn't so lucky. He needed a break of some kind, and if J. T.'s offer was it, he couldn't afford to pass it up just because he didn't like the terms.

"I don't know," Jesse said. "I'm not sure my back could take it."

"I tell you what," J. T. said. "It's the Stavely Stampede today. Let's take a run up there. You try it out, and I'll have a look at you. Then we'll decide."

[*32*]

The idea appealed to Jesse. There wouldn't be anybody at the Stavely show—all the name cowboys and best bucking stock were in Cheyenne this week. Jesse could slip in quietly and try his spurs on some old cayuse against a bunch of novices. It wouldn't cost him anything, and who could tell—they might even win a couple of bucks. "Okay," Jesse said. "And then we'll decide."

C H A P T E R   V

BY the time they came out of the beer parlor, Jesse felt that simply by pushing with his feet he could turn the world whichever way he wanted, like a bear on a medicine ball. There wasn't a man he couldn't lick; there wasn't a horse he couldn't ride. Bring him as big a horse as you wanted, as black as you could find. Jesse would ride him down to the size of a baby pig—till the saddle slipped off him and Jesse rolled on the ground, and the tiny horse ran off, all pink and white.

They got in the Dodge and started off for Stavely forty miles to the north. "You're a lucky man, John Tyler Jones," Jesse said. "I don't know why you should be, but you are. It just happens that today you have made the best deal of your life. How could you tell I got a special gift? When I was just a kid I could watch a horse's ears and tell what he'd be like to ride. Before I straddled him I knew just what was coming, and when it came, my bones knew what to do, like they were born to it. It came to me natural as riding a woman." Jesse's mouth seemed so full of words that if he didn't let some of them out he'd choke.

To the west he could see the Porcupine Hills, with the

very tops of the distant mountains just showing above them. Under the wheels of the Dodge, though, the ground rushed by as flat as a rug, as though the wind had worn away every rock, leveled every hump and undulation that may ever have been there. The swails and hills were gone, but the wind remained. Occasional gusts shook the car.

"I thought the wind blew out on Milk River Ridge," Jesse said. "But that wasn't a schoolmarm's whistle to what they got here today."

"Every day," J.T. told him. "One time the wind stopped blowing in Macleod, and everybody in town fell over."

Jesse hadn't meant to change the subject. "Yes sir, J. T., I've got a gift. Today there's not an animal dressed in horsehide that I can't fan till his tail drops off. That's one thing about it. I got a gift. I can feel what's goin' to happen. I can feel it in my bones that today I could ride any damn bronc you care to name right up the side of them mountains."

Midnight was the horse that killed Pete Knight. Jesse wasn't scared of Midnight. He'd ride him to the top of the mountain and back again. "Next week is the Macleod Stampede. Then Raymond, and Calgary. You're in for a summer, J. T., I tell you that. I don't know who's going to put up your hay."

"Let's see what happens today."

"You can hire Indians to put up your hay. With what you'll be making, you could hire the Prince of Wales and still be money ahead, eh, pardner?"

"We're not partners yet," J. T. reminded him. "Not till you fan that first bronc, at least."

"Don't worry," Jesse said. "You want to worry, worry about rain on your fresh-cut hay, but don't you worry about me."

The road was straight as a meridian, leading them down into the north, where the distant prairie was blurred by the wind and blowing dust. The sun gave the dust an amber tinge, so the earth seemed wrapped in clouds of powdered gold. While they were still miles away, the elevators at Stavely rose out of the mists, three great square-shouldered sentinels, sounding the alarm: "Jesse Gifford's coming! Sixteen feet high, with eyes like furnace doors. Iron skin and granite bones. Run, you cowboys! Hide your children. Jesse Gifford's coming!"

Stavely was a thin Y of dirt roads set against the railway track, with stunted trees and houses as gray as the road. Today the town was filled with people. People walking, people in cars, people on horseback, floating up and down, waving banners, honking horns. People looking in the window of J. T.'s Dodge; looking at the man in the passenger's seat: Jesse Gifford.

"I need a drink," Jesse said.

"Getting nervous?" J. T. asked. "You don't have to worry. Nobody'll remember you."

"We've got time to stop at the hotel for a minute."

"I'd say you got just about the right mix now to make you pliable without turning limp. Besides, we've got to get out to the grounds and register you. We're not up here on a pleasure jaunt, you know."

No. This is strictly a business proposition—you break your neck, Jesse Gifford, and I'll still be here to spend what you win. How's that for a business proposition? But it costs me. Look at what it's cost me already. Just getting you drunk so you won't turn tail and run the last minute. Look, J. T. You didn't have to get me drunk. There ain't a thing on earth, man or beast, that I'm scared of. Then there's the entrance fee, Jesse. And the gas to drive you up here. And what I'd be worth if I'd stayed home and worked. Plus the

[*35*]

wages I'm paying you. I'm putting plenty into this partnership, and all I can say is you'd better win.

The car pulled up on the grass behind the grandstand. Jesse opened the door, climbed out, and stretched on his toes with his hands above his head. Twenty feet high, with arms like bear traps. Arms for crushing or holding. If Keno, then to crush; if Shirley, just to hold, with jaws that would not bruise her but would never let her go.

J. T. walked like a two-legged puppy dog, and Jesse came behind, the people swirling around his knees like water. Jesse strode into them, down into the stampede river. Four years without a breath. Here I am. I've come to breathe again the stampede air, rich and heavy as a river.

Young cowboys with thumbs in belts and legs apart laugh and smoke, and stare at old men's eyes like they were stones in a museum case. They give their names to the man who keeps the book—an angel writing in a book of gold, and Jesse Gifford's name leads all the rest.

Sound and color, dust and turmoil; cowboys swinging small looped lariats against the wind; bucking bulls with bells a-clanging; names called through a megaphone—names nobody heard of. Moaning horses wrapped in yellow chaps, horses made with stiff front legs for stamping hoofprints in the earth; other cowboys, old and broken, hanging on, the scars of their bodies showing in their eyes. "Hello, Jesse. What you doin' here?" "Got hungry for a bit of gravel."

More painful to be remembered than forgotten. Jesse Gifford shrinks. Hands in pockets, he pulls up to hold himself tall, but still he shrinks. A kid in yellow chaps down into the chute, down onto a saddle cinched to the back of Blue Angel. The man with the megaphone says, "Jack Tatum on Blue Angel!" His voice trails off to the east like smoke. The clang of the chute, and Blue Angel floats out like a dancer, shoulders high, wrapped in yellow chaps, lands with a jolt that breaks the kid loose from his saddle, his hat loose from his head; still he clings, riding her neck it seems, first on one side, then the other; the kid is clear, spread-eagled, floating, shirt a-flutter in the wind; Blue Angel goes her way alone, still faintly bucking; the pickup men, not needed now, follow her to the gate; the horn sounds, too late, and men in white coats pick the kid out of the dust; he pushes them away, legs in yellow chaps grope for the ground beneath, shift to try to make the world hold still; he walks toward the chutes, the crowd stands up to cheer.

Breathe that air: the stampede air thick with the dread of blood, but hungry for it; the same air used for cheers by people in the stands, but wasted on them; thick air that turns to solid grit when cowboys breathe it.

Jesse smaller now, pulling at his belt, but shrinking from inside where he can't reach it, gulping at the stampede air. He's scareder than a kid. Scared of what? Not scared to die—a hoof right in his heart won't worry him—but scared of pain, of broken bones and months in bed; scared of young men's laughing eyes if he gets piled; scared most of all he's finished—that he'll go home broke and never ride again. Better he should be killed; death or glory, that was it—no middle ground. The shrinking stops. He grows a bit again. He'll show those young yahoos what riding is.

"Jesse Gifford riding Calico! Chute number two!" Down in chute number two they're tightening the cinch around old Calico—jugheaded, long as a noodle; no doubt pulled a hay rake yesterday. What can he do today? Down in the saddle, boots in stirrups. Calico's long neck raised, his head turned slightly, with one eye looking back; Jesse's hand as short on the rope as it can get, right hand pulling down his hat. "Let 'er go!" The chute slams open, Calico stands still. Jesse suddenly hot, wild, feverish, insane, raises his spurs beside old Calico's neck. "Trample me, you dirty gray old eunuch. Trample me, you bastard!" The spurs, descending, rake the matted hair from neck to belly, Calico plunges in the chute, slams against the planks, turns, pivots and comes apart, legs and neck in all direction; grandstand turns dizzily passed, chutes, horses, ground spin by in jagged blurs, Jesse showing daylight, riding loose, raking Calico all the while—like riding a bicycle, you never forget how. "Wa-hoo!" He'd ride old Calico right over the mountains.

The saddle came up against him, hard, jarring his bones like a sack of rocks. Suddenly he'd lost his rhythm. Before he could recover, Calico rolled out and left him alone with only a halter rope in his hand. It pulled him straight down, slammed him on the ground, and he could see Calico's underparts stretched above him. He rolled, and the earth beneath his head shook when the great hooves landed. If he'd laid still, it would all be over now. He wouldn't have to get up like it didn't hurt, and wave at the cheering crowd, and smile, and walk back to the chutes.

J. T. Jones, standing beside him, cursed. "Let's go home," he said.

CHAPTER VI

MONDAY was another long day, made longer for Jesse when he finally went to bed and found that he couldn't sleep. It might have been the pain in his back that kept him awake, but toward midnight it had almost subsided, and still he lay, turning over the day's events like carcasses in his mind.

The morning had begun for him on the iron seat of J. T.'s tractor, with the cold iron wheel in his hands and a cultivator lurching after him. The west wind blew from the mountains. The exhaust of the tractor came from a vertical pipe in front of him, and the dust rose in a cloud from the cultivator behind him, so that whichever way he faced in his traverse of the field, he seemed to ride in a pall of acrid fumes or choking dust. Sometimes the tractor lugs broke through the crust of the earth, and sometimes they were held up by it, so that the machine seemed to progress by intermittent jolts and thrusts, and hesitations. Almost from the beginning, his back began to hurt.

Ethan had wanted to start school, even though summer vacation was less than a week away. As the sun climbed and the wind grew warmer, Jesse saw the boys ride off on the pinto toward the white schoolhouse that stood on a hill three miles away. That meant it was not yet nine. Already his back felt like six-day misery, but he was determined to last till suppertime.

Presently the cultivator began to collect remnants of stubble mixed with the weed and thistles that covered the field, and Jesse looked back to see the rubbish packing so tightly beneath the frame that it was lifting the blades out of the ground. He stopped the outfit. He must have spent half an hour hacking at the impacted stalks with his pocket-knife, tugging at them straw by straw, until finally, first at one shaft and then the next, one by one, the debris crumbled and fell away, and he was able to continue. Almost at once the trailing straws and stems began to catch on the cultivator shafts again. Jesse watched closely. This time he would not let the mess get so solidly imbedded before he cleared it. In fact, he watched the cultivator so closely that he didn't see the big rock until it was too late, and just as he depressed the clutch, the outfit jerked to a shuddering stop, a wheel and one blade of the cultivator neatly straddling the rock. It appeared that as yet nothing was broken. However, if he tried to pull the machine from where it was stuck, something would have to give, and it wouldn't be the rock. What he needed was a jack.

He walked across the field and over the hill to J. T.'s farmyard. The dog barked as he approached, but apparently J. T. was not around. In the shop he found a lumber jack that must have weighed thirty pounds. Holding it in one hand, he started to walk quickly back up the hill. When he got to the top, where he could see the field, he set the jack down and stood there breathing hard. The tractor was so far away it looked about the size of a spool of thread. The way that jack pried against his innards when he lifted it, he thought the old pelvis was coming right apart. He could leave the jack where it was, go and unhitch the tractor and bring it over to carry the jack on. But if J. T. should see him do that, he would wonder what was happening, and Jesse hoped that J. T. would never find out about this little mishap.

He started across the field, carrying the jack first in one hand, and then the other, and stopping frequently to rest. For a while he wasn't sure he'd make it. He thought he might just have to leave the jack there in the middle of the field. If he did that, however, the only thing left for him would be to load his trappings on his horse, pick up the boys at school, and head out for somewhere far enough away that he'd never see John Tyler Jones again. That thought—of setting out again—filled him with such despair that he continued across the field and eventually reached the tractor.

[*40*]

He set the jack down beside the cultivator and lay back on the hard, lumpy ground, his arm thrown across his face to shield his eyes from the sun. Gradually the pain in his back subsided.

He raised himself. So far this morning he had completed two and a half rounds of the field. J. T. wouldn't think much of that for a morning's work. He set the jack under the frame of the cultivator right beside the rock. Then by repeatedly pushing the jack handle down until the dog slipped in place, then raising and pushing it down again, the end of the cultivator was raised by slow degrees until the wheel was perhaps eight inches clear of the ground.

He heard a sound approaching, and turned to see the boys riding toward him on the pinto. They rode up close, and stopped. "Keep away," he said. "Stay right back away. Why aren't you kids in school?"

"The teacher sent us home," Ethan replied.

"What do you mean, she sent you home?"

"She said George is too young for school. She says she didn't go to normal school to be a baby tender."

"George isn't a baby."

"Well, he's never been to school before. And here it is only a week till summer holidays."

At Gillespie's there had always been one of the women willing to look after George. They'd do anything for George and Ethan—bake cookies for them and mend their overalls. They treated them like a couple of orphans.

"She says I can come," Ethan went on. "But I had to bring George home."

"Well, leave him here," Jesse said. "He'll be all right with me."

George swung over the side of the pinto, with his arms around his brother's waist, his small bare feet stretched down toward the ground. Then he dropped. Ethan turned and galloped away, back toward the schoolhouse.

"Now, keep away," Jesse said. "Stand clear back there." George backed two steps across the cultivated ground. He stared at the jack with its slim shaft poised under the iron and stone weight of the cultivator. "Further back," Jesse said. "Further." George backed again, tripped and fell down, stood up, brushed his hands on the legs of his overalls, his eyes on the jack. Jesse knelt down and tried to judge with his eye whether the cultivator would clear the rock now. It looked as if it would.

At the front of the tractor a permanent crank hung out like the tongue of a dog. Jesse primed the machine by filling the sediment bowl, bent and seized the crank and gave it a quick turn. There was a sucking *pop*, a ball of blue smoke shot into the air, and then everything was quiet again.

"It almost started," George said.

Jesse turned the crank again. He got the same response. The machine had started with one turn of the crank for J. T. that morning. He tried again, and again. It gave evidence of life but showed no interest in becoming fully animated. At last, in desperation, Jesse seized the crank in both hands and spun it as fast as he could. Normally he was cautious while cranking a tractor. He considered it more dangerous than a wild horse. But as his exasperation increased, his caution faded, and just at the moment when pain and anger had driven any awareness of hazard from his mind, the tractor backfired. The crank reversed direction, snapping back with such sudden force that before he could let go of it, Jesse was thrown to the ground. His left thumb and wrist felt as though they were broken.

George came running over beside him. He squatted down, looking into Jesse's face. "It kicked you."

[42]

Jesse didn't want to be looked at just then. He was about to send George home alone when he heard another voice, and glanced up to see John Tyler Jones surveying the situation. "Did you set the magneto?" J. T. asked. He pulled, or pushed, something on the tractor, turned the crank—he looked too small for the job—there was a sudden eruption of noise and smoke, J. T. throttled it down, and the machine stood there idling. Its fenders rattled, as if impatient to get back to work.

When J. T. swung up on the tractor seat, Jesse rose and moved to one side. J. T. put the machine in low, and with his head turned back to watch the cultivator, he slowly let out the clutch. The cultivator moved perhaps an inch, and stopped. The jack had begun to tilt. "Is it going to make it?" J. T. shouted.

Jesse bent down to look at the cultivator shoes poised above the rock. Actually, he didn't care if it made it or not. Right then his wrist and thumb were hurting so bad he couldn't think of anything else. "I think so," he said. He motioned George back. J. T. moved forward another inch, then another, another. The jack tipped, thrusting the cultivator forward against the clevis that joined it to the tractor, the blade rang against the rock and glanced forward. The jack fell. In spite of his pain, Jesse felt a sense of relief. At least they were over the rock.

J. T. jumped down from the tractor, picked up the jack, and set it in the metal well between the shuddering fenders of the machine. He walked over to Jesse. "You hurt yourself?" he asked loudly, above the noise of the tractor.

"I'll be all right," Jesse said. "Just sprained my wrist."

"You'd better go home and soak it," J. T. said. "I'll run the outfit."

"No. I'm all right."

"At the rate you're going, it'll take you a week to finish this field. I haven't that much time."

"I've never run a tractor very much," Jesse said.

"No wonder!" J. T. exclaimed. He climbed on the tractor again. Then he glanced back at Jesse. "I'll work late to catch up!" he shouted. "You milk my cow, will you?" The tractor started forward. J. T. opened the throttle wide, the noise rose up like the dust from the cultivator, and the outfit moved slowly away, its roar punctuated by a chorus of shrieks as the steel-pointed shoes struck against the stones of the field.

Now, lying there in the dark, wide awake, Jesse tried to think where it was, in the course of that single day, that he had gone wrong. Actually, it was J. T.'s fault. He ought to take a stoneboat out there and haul that rock away. Still, J. T. had treated him like a fool, and made him milk the cow for punishment. He wished he hadn't milked her. All afternoon he'd lain on his bed thinking about that cow, nursing his sprained wrist and giving his back a chance to recuperate from the punishment it had received that morning. All afternoon he lay there thinking, about J. T. and the cow, and San Soucie and old Lars, and the fact that though he wasn't yet thirty-five, everybody looked at him as if he was already another Lars. They saw him not as a man, but as someone who used to be one.

George had played around the yard outside the bedroom window, and presently Ethan came home from school. The boys walked in and out of the room as if it contained a corpse. At suppertime Ethan cut some bread and fixed syrup sandwiches. Jesse wasn't hungry. He went over to J. T.'s to milk the cow. It took him a long time because he could milk with only one hand.

Later on, Ethan came in and sat on the bed across from

him. "George told me you got fired today," he said.

"I didn't get fired."

"Are you still working for J. T.?"

"As far as I know."

"How are you going to work with a bad back?"

"I'll be all right, come haying time."

"What happens after haying's finished?" Ethan's face had little smears of syrup on each cheek, like an inspector's stamp certifying its youth. His eyes, though, were old. There was mystery in them, but there was weariness too, as though already the earth held nothing more he wished to see.

"Haven't we always gotten along somehow?" Jesse said.

"I guess we have," the boy agreed. "Somehow." He paused. "I'm scared, Jesse. What's going to happen to us?" For a long time he looked at the floor. When he looked at Jesse again, he said, "I always wondered why Mama left us." He stood up. Then he blurted, "I think I know now," and ran out of the house; each pounding footstep seemed to land square in the middle of Jesse's back.

Now again, in the middle of the night, the pain gushed up in him, crushing his spirit against the walls of his body until he knew he could not endure it. This was not a physical pain; it was the pain of disappointment, old and unremitting, but in the days with Shirley, so softened by the sweet smoke of love that he had never really noticed it. What's going to happen to us?

The solution came quite naturally. Perhaps it was not a perfect idea, but it arrived with an irresistible force that seemed to confirm its rightness. As he lay there in the dark, the events of the day fell upon him like stones thrown on a grave, and suddenly he realized that a grave was where he belonged—someplace where he couldn't feel the weight of the stones. He would hang himself.

He threw back the covers and sat up on the side of his bed. There was a moon, and its light reflected enough from the whitewashed wall that he could make out the faces of the boys, round and innocent, turned to the window. It seemed the final irony that the best thing he could do for them was leave them to Keno. He had taken Jesse's title, and Jesse's woman, and now he would get Jesse's boys.

Quietly he began to dress. This kind of thinking would blur the clearness of his intent. He must act quickly.

As he passed through the kitchen he saw the outline of the syrup can on the table. He hadn't had any supper, and he was hungry. He took the heel of the loaf from the bread drawer, and was about to cut it when he realized that he was stealing his sons' inheritance. "And to my sons, Ethan and George, I leave a quarter of a loaf of bread and a can of Roger's Golden Syrup." Hah! For a moment he even considered starting a fire and frying a couple of eggs as well. But then he realized that ridiculous as it seemed, his off-the-cuff testament was true. In his spare estate, food for the morning's breakfast would be a generous part. He'd lost his appetite, anyway. He returned the bread to the drawer and hurried out of the house.

The dry sunflower stalks beside the path to the stable were five feet tall, heads drooping, black as mourners. As Jesse walked along, his elbow brushed their leaves, causing them to rustle softly. It was the only sound he could hear.

There was a moment just before he reached the stable when he wanted to stop and think this thing through, but he knew if he did, he would end up doing nothing. Just once before he died, he wanted to hold a course of action firmly to its conclusion.

First he got his lariat. Its coil felt hard as a cable in his hand, as though it would be more inclined to cut than to jerk. He had heard that the hangman's art was not a simple one. If the drop was too short, the neck would not be broken, and the poor devil would have to hang there until he strangled. But if the drop was too long, it might pull his head off. It all had to be carefully worked out in relation to the victim's height, weight, bone and muscle structure, and perhaps collar size for all Jesse knew. Add to this the difference in thickness between a hangman's noose and a lariat loop, and Jesse saw that his chances of hitting on the right formula were pretty slim. Still, in the old days they hanged men from cottonwood trees by the dozen, and whipped their horses out from under them, and Jesse had never heard of it jerking anybody's head off. The important thing was to drop far enough—he didn't fancy hanging there in the moonlight waiting to choke to death.

He had considered using his horse in the classic tradition, but it seemed to add another variable and to draw Czar into complicity in an act which he would not approve. Besides, as he stood outside the stable, Jesse looked up and saw a ready-made gallows—the high roof beam of the loft, standing bare and gaunt against the brilliant sky. There was a hole in the barn ceiling directly beneath the beam, designed as a feeder hole when the loft was finished and filled with hay. All he had to do was climb up to the floor of the loft, tie the lariat to the roof beam, calculate the length of drop he needed, put the loop around his neck, and step off into the feed hole. It would give him a drop of at least eight feet, which he was sure would be ample.

He went into the stable. The interior was dark, except for a square in the center where the light through the feeder hole fell on the bars of the ladder that led up through it. He groped his way to the ladder and began to climb, the coil of the rope around his shoulder. There came to his mind a strong inclination to use the shotgun and avoid the uncertainties of hanging. He resisted it, climbing the ladder step by step as the jack had raised the cultivator. That decision had worked—the one to get the jack—and with unaccustomed clarity of vision, he knew that this one would too. Strange, that only now, at the very end of his life, did he seem to feel any control over it. The sense of mastery was too sweet to dilute by indecision. He reached the top and walked onto the floor of the loft. The old boards gleamed like silver, with the shadow of the roof beam lying on them as black as paint.

He threw the loop of the lariat over the beam and tied the other end to a log joist that extended at the side. He tested the rope, lifting himself off the floor on it. So far as he could tell, he was ready.

It seemed that something else was required. A few last words? Who was there to hear them? A prayer? Would God listen to him at a time like this? A moment of silence? There would soon be plenty of that. This was just another stall. He stood beside the feed hole and raised the loop until it was even with his eyes. Perhaps in his lifetime he had thrown ten thousand loops around ten thousand necks—cows' necks, calves' necks, horses' necks, dogs' necks . . . He'd even roped a chicken once, with a loop not much bigger than the one he now held.

This was the last loop of all, around his own neck. He raised his Stetson just long enough to pass the loop over his head. He buttoned his shirt collar and turned it up, pulling the loop snug on the outside of it.

It was possible that halfway down, his resolve might waver; even involuntarily he might spread his arms and catch himself on the sides of the feed hole, or worse yet, only break the fall so that the rope wouldn't do its work in one quick snap. He was not simple enough to suppose that by an exercise of will alone he could prevent this. He would have to do something with his arms. If he could worm both hands into his pockets at the same time, and then double up his fists, his arms would be anchored like the little boy in the cookie jar. He slipped his left hand into the pocket first, then his right, which found the pocketknife and gathered it into its palm. The metal parts of the knife were cold against his skin. He realized his palms were wet. He seemed to notice for the first time a roaring in his ears which had started there he couldn't say when.

What if death really didn't end everything? What if all that was left was this roaring in his ears, and it went on for ever and ever? He knew a man whose leg had been amputated, and the toes of that foot were always cold. The man said he could feel his toes down there, and wiggle them, but when he sat by the fire, there was nothing to absorb the heat, and empty air just went on paining him with horrible ghostly cold. Suppose death was like that—just an endless roar in ears that didn't exist? With an effort, he called himself back to his purpose. He had begun to shiver. Had he delayed too long? Jesse jumped into the hole.

Falling. Wind and roar and rushing shadows. He didn't want to die. He knew it now. He'd been mistaken. He saw the black square gulping him—his knees, his hips, his waist. Oh, fool! Oh, damn, dead, dangling fool! His hands were free—too late. His boots shot out and broke the ladder rungs like match sticks—then caught and held. His hands reached up and seized the rope above his head. The ladder wavered beneath his toe; then, with a screech, a nail that held it to the joist pulled loose, and his support gave way.

[*49*]

Jesse swung free, his weight hanging from his hands gripped on the lariat above his head.

It was dark in the stable. He kicked about in hope of finding some hold, and his boot came against the remains of the ladder, hanging loose, so that wherever he pushed against it, it moved away. He tried to climb hand over hand, but his arms were aching already, and his fingers numb, as if they might let the rope slip away from them at any moment.

He began to shout, as loud as he could. The word he repeated was "Ethan," but was so distorted by the force and rhythm of his voice that it was scarcely distinguishable. "E-e-th-a-a-n!" he cried. "E-e-th-a-a-n!" It was a desperate hope that he could waken one of the boys, but he could think of no other. What a crazy way to die.

Ethan's white body appeared in the darkness beneath him, naked except for his shorts. Jesse's shout trailed off and stopped. There was a moment of eerie silence.

"Quick," Jesse gasped. "Get me something to stand on."

The boy sucked in his breath.

"Quick," Jesse cried again. "I'm falling."

Ethan tried to gather Jesse's dangling legs into his arms and lift. He was only making it worse.

"Get a box!" Jesse said. He had no idea himself where a box might be.

"Stick your legs up," Ethan said.

Help had arrived, but what kind of help was this? Stick your legs up! "I'm going to fall," Jesse puffed. "Get something for me to stand on."

"Flip over," Ethan said. "Flip on your head and put your legs through this hole."

Jesse couldn't figure out what the kid was talking about.

He kicked futilely toward the hole above him.

"You don't have to kick," Ethan said. "Just turn your body upside down on the rope. Just swing your whole body. Us kids used to do it on the rope at the swimming hole."

He made it sound so simple. Well, Jesse would fire his last bolt of strength in one more effort, and Ethan would learn too late that life was not so simple as he thought. With a paroxysm that felt as if it would break his arms, Jesse inverted his body, and found himself head down, with his legs in the air. When they fell back they landed on the edge of the hole. He felt an instant of stunned amazement, almost as great as his relief. It had been easy, almost like magic. With one swift motion, he pulled the top part of his body level with his legs, jerked the noose from his head, and rolled onto the floor of the loft.

CHAPTER VII

THEY went to bed, each as silent as if he were alone. Jesse didn't expect to sleep, but he was tired, with an unfamiliar kind of weariness. Almost at once, he fell asleep.

When he first opened his eyes in the morning, Jesse didn't remember the events of the night before. He had been dreaming something, and for a moment he lay musing on what it might have been. When recollection came, it was not of the dream, but of reality. Slowly, like a leak in a dike, he started to remember, and then the whole thing gave way and with a rush the full weight of his guilt fell over him. To hang himself! To have bungled the job was even worse, and to have Ethan find him was the most terrible of all. The sunlight coming through the window was a cheerful obscenity, like a brass band at a funeral.

The boys' bed was empty. Just as well. He didn't feel ready to face Ethan yet. Had things gone slightly otherwise, he'd be dead by now, and would never have to face him. His body would be dead, hanging from a rope in the barn, and when Ethan found it he'd start to scream. Only Jesse wouldn't hear the scream if he were dead.

Somewhere outside the window he heard the boys' voices, intermittent and low. He couldn't tell what they were saying. As long as Ethan wasn't telling George about what happened last night, he didn't care. Surely, though, Ethan would be as anxious to forget it as Jesse. Perhaps they could go on as if nothing had happened, and never mention it again.

Jesse sat up on the side of the bed, took his hat from a nail on the wall, and put it on his head. That was the right approach, of course, to go on as if last night had been only a dream. It might be difficult for Ethan to do, but he was a bright boy—he would understand that it was the only way they could go on at all. There was no need for George to ever know anything about it.

The boys' talk sounded matter-of-fact, natural, unexcited. Jesse was relieved. Ethan would forgive him. He was lucky to have such a son; one could save his life and then not hold it over him.

Come to think of it, this experience might help Ethan —might even be good for him. He had never shown much patience with the problems Jesse faced. Obviously he had no idea of their force or complexity. What could a kid know about missing the championship by a whisper, or having

[52]

your woman run out on you? Sometimes Ethan talked as though all Jesse had to do was punch San Soucie in the nose and shoot Keno in the gut, and his troubles would be over. If only it were that simple. Well, perhaps this would impress Ethan with how overwhelming life can be, even to a grown man. If he was unable to comprehend the details, maybe now at least he would show some respect for what he couldn't understand.

There was another sound out there besides the youthful quiet voices—a *shuck, swish* sound repeated over and over, as if someone were digging. Jesse pulled on his overalls and walked barefoot through the kitchen, buttoning his shirt as he went. In the yard he stopped short. At the center of an old weed-grown garden plot not far from the house, Ethan stood knee-deep in a hole he was digging. George sprawled on a dirt pile beside him. Jesse tucked in his shirt. Then he walked toward them.

George fell silent, and turned his head to stare at Jesse. Ethan went right on working. His hole was about the size of a door. On one ranch where they lived, an older boy had dug himself a cave, covered it with boards, and then placed sod on top, with a trap door to get in and out. Ethan, much younger then, had been enchanted by that cave, and vowed some day he would dig one of his own. This must be it.

"Good morning, boys," Jesse said as he approached. They did not reply, but Ethan paused in his work and looked at Jesse. The pause started to become awkward, and it was important to keep things casual—matter-of-fact—as if nothing had happened. "What are you doing?" Jesse asked.

"Digging a grave," Ethan replied.

"Oh." Digging a grave. As calmly as if he were making a ditch. Digging a grave. Jesse made one more effort to turn things back in their old channel, where nothing had happened. A laugh might do it, if he could find one. "Did your pet walrus die?" he asked. Nobody laughed. But George looked solemnly up at him and said, "It's for you." For Jesse. A grave for Jesse. "But I'm not dead," he told them. Ethan began to dig again. "We want to be ready."

With two steps Jesse was into the hole, seized the shovel in one hand, and with the other slapped Ethan's face so hard that the boy stumbled across the hole, tripped on the edge of it, and fell heavily on the pile of dirt. Jesse felt as if all the blood in his body had risen and begun to beat inside his head. He became aware that he was standing over his son, with the shovel held in both hands like a weapon. Ethan's eyes stared back at him, cool and black, unafraid, like Shirley's eyes.

Shirley coming home to Gillespie's late at night, cool and black and unafraid—black dress, black hair, black eyes, black heart. Shirley walking down the road from God knew where, softly singing; singing to the whole countryside if they cared to listen; singing softly, with a voice so rich and low it seemed to come out of her belly. Perhaps even singing to Jesse there in the cottage, still slumped in his old wicker chair, staring straight ahead as he had been when the sun went down. Shirley opening the screen door at one o'clock in the morning, cool and black and unafraid, singing. Shirley standing against the light of the doorway, in slim black dress and high-heeled shoes. Shirley faceless, black against the moonlight through the door. "Aren't you in bed yet?"

All the words he had prepared now suddenly rubbish, clogging his throat in a tangled lump.

"You didn't have to wait up," she said.

"I wondered what happened to you."

"I went for a walk."

In high-heeled shoes, she went for a walk. "George was home alone. I thought something must have happened."

"George wasn't alone. Ethan was here."

"Ethan got home from school late tonight. When I came in, George was alone."

Shirley striking a match, lighting a cigarette; Shirley, who never smoked. In the flare of the match he had seen her eyes—cool, black, and unafraid. "Blame Ethan then. Don't blame me."

"I'm not blaming you." But he had been. George, four years old, alone in the cottage. Why hadn't she lied to him, at least? She could have told him she didn't leave until Ethan got home. Then it would have been her word against Ethan's. That was the terrible part of it—that she didn't even care enough to lie about it. No doubt if he asked her where she'd been, she'd have told him that, too. "I was worried about you," he said.

"Very touching." Shirley going to the bedroom, kicking off her shoes, stripping, her body white and curved and slender in the moonlight. "What's the matter? Didn't you ever see a naked woman before?"

Jesse in the doorway, watching her—watching her white skin, as white as the first snow of winter—magic snow that didn't reveal the tracks of wild animals crushing it beneath their paws. He longed to touch that cool, soft snow himself, that magic snow. He walked toward her. She slipped her nightgown over her head. When he came close he saw her eyes, cool as the magic snow, black as the snow was white.

"Shirley," he said.

[55]

"Don't touch me!"

Now Ethan's eyes looked up at him, black and unafraid. Jesse lowered the shovel and sat down on the edge of the hole. His bare feet were white and ugly against the dirt. "What do you mean?" he asked. "You want to be ready?"

"For when you kill yourself," Ethan replied. He raised himself and sat on the other side of the hole, across from Jesse. His eyes were still steady, still cool, looking at his father.

"I'm not going to kill myself," Jesse said.

It was difficult for Ethan to talk without revealing a catch in his voice, but he did the best he could. "You tried last night."

"I won't do it again."

"How do I know that? Did you think about me and George? What would happen to us?"

"'Mama would take care of you."

"Yah!" It came out as a sob, and Ethan had to pause to gain control of his voice. "Mama and Keno! You want us to live with Keno?"

"You'd be better off."

For a few minutes Ethan did not try to speak again. Then he said, more calmly, "I couldn't go to sleep last night. I just laid awake, thinking. And, Jesse, you're not going to kill yourself. That's what I decided." He paused again, but Jesse did not speak. "If you do," he went on at last, "if you do kill yourself, George and I aren't going to tell anybody. We're going to bury you in this hole, and tell everybody you just went away. You just rode away and never told us where you were going. That's what we'll say. And after Mama comes to get us and take us to live with Keno, those Indian dogs will come across the river and start sniffing around. And they'll dig you up and eat you and

scatter your bones all over the bloody ranch." Ethan
choked. Then he went on. "If you kill yourself, that's what
we'll do. And that's what will happen. And you won't be
here to stop it." Ethan paused, then added, "So, if that's
what you want, you just go ahead and kill yourself."
He stood up and walked away, down the path toward
the stable. George looked at his father. He scrambled off the
dirt pile and got to his feet. Still looking at Jesse, he brushed
his hands against his pant legs. Then he turned and ran
after Ethan, over the fence, through the pasture, and into
the trees that grew beside the river.

CHAPTER VIII

THE morning air clung around Jesse, hot and motionless,
but he could still feel under his bare feet the cool damp
earth at the bottom of his grave. His grave. How many men
had a grave all ready and waiting for them? Even John D.
Rockefeller would have to die before anybody dug a grave
for him. Jesse felt a strong inclination to lie down and pull
the dirt over him. It seemed like the perfect ending. But
somehow life didn't end, it just went blundering on. He
knew now he'd live to be a hundred if he could; every breath
a curse, and every step a misery, he'd cling to life till there
was nothing left to hang on to. He rose, picked up the
shovel, and began to push the dirt back into his grave.
There was no use leaving it open to the weather like this.
All he had to do now was figure out some way to endure. When he thought of fifty more years of life on the
earth, he shuddered. This morning he couldn't face it
alone. He needed people around him, people who didn't

know him, people who wouldn't look at him and say, "Poor old Jesse Gifford." He needed to look somebody in the eye that wouldn't laugh at him and think: You silly old saddle-tramp. Somebody that would look at him and say, "You must be a cowboy, mister." "Yes sir, I'm a cowboy. I'm the best bronc rider in the world." He might find somebody like that in Lethbridge. The question was—how would he get there? It was an all-day ride on horseback. J. T. wouldn't take him, that was certain. He was marooned.

Far above him a hawk soared, screaming intermittently. A breeze rustled the dry sunflower stalks that stood behind the grave. For a moment, then, the morning seemed absolutely still, and in the stillness he heard a train whistle. Tuesday morning! Train day! That was the warning whistle. Lone Rock to Lethbridge. Rescued.

He'd have to hurry. He ran into the house, and while he pulled on his socks and boots he glanced about him. It was possible that he might never come back. What was there to come back for? The boys would be happy to have him gone, without even the trouble of a burial. He'd never stop missing them—as he still missed Shirley—but there was certainly nothing else here that he couldn't either carry with him or leave behind and never feel a twinge.

A half-hour. That was all the time he had, and catching that train was more important than any single item he might forget. Old Czar would have to run for it. Well, that wouldn't hurt him as a final friendly gesture to his old master. He did pause when he thought of Czar. He could take his saddle and bridle on the train with him, but it would be good-bye to Czar. He'd probably end up in Keno's horse pasture.

Fully dressed, Jesse slipped on his denim jumper and took his sheepskin coat from a nail. He put his picture of

Shirley in one jumper pocket, shotgun shells in the other, took the gun in his hand, and ran out the door. He dropped his coat beside the stable door, grabbed the bridle, and hurried to the pasture to catch Czar. He was halfway across the field before he realized he still had the shotgun in his hand. Damn. He couldn't put it down in the wet grass. What had possessed him, anyway, that he didn't just leave it with the sheepskin coat? Well, no matter. It wouldn't slow him down. He hurried on to where his two horses grazed peacefully, the color of their coats heightened, it seemed, by the sparkle of the dewy grass in which they stood. As Jesse approached, the pinto raised his head. Then Czar looked back across his shoulder and nickered softly. Funny. At the very last, Czar was the only friend he had in the world.

As he ran up to the horse, he spoke to him softly. "Czar old boy, we've got a race to run this morning." He raised the bridle. With a toss of his head, Czar snorted and moved out of reach. "Whoa, boy. We've got no time for games." He never had any trouble catching Czar, but he'd never run up to him before, either. Jesse took a deep breath. Just for a moment, till he got that head-stall fastened, he'd have to take it slow. "Whoa, boy." He walked forward, his hand stretched out toward Czar's neck. "Thata boy. Whoa, fella," his voice was soft. Czar looked at him, snorted, and moved away. "Whoa, boy." It must be the shotgun that was scaring him; perhaps it looked to him like a club. Now, as Jesse approached again, Czar arched his neck with lowered head and broke into a trot. "Whoa, boy. Whoa." Jesse ran after him. The fence was close by. He could catch him there.

The shotgun, next to his horse and saddle, was his prize possession. He didn't use it much, but the barrel was scrolled with a symmetry that pleased his heart each time he looked at it, and the stock hand-carved so that embossed flowers seemed to grow backward from the grip. He had won it on a bet, and while his other possessions seemed to drop off on the trail behind him like lizard skins, he was always careful to keep his shotgun. Now he was simply putting it down in the grass. He'd have plenty of time to wipe it off and oil it on the train to Lethbridge. He leaned it against a gopher hole so the barrel slanted upward slightly, just enough that he'd be able to find it again. Then he started after Czar, who by now was standing against the fence, looking back at him. "Whoa, fella. Whoa, boy."

Jesse found himself half running again. Time was getting short, but he forced himself to slow down. With a quick, gliding pace, half walk, half run, he hurried toward Czar, but as he came closer, he slowed still more. "There you are, boy. Quiet now, fella. Easy does it. Thata boy. Whoa, boy. Whoa, fella." Czar moved a few paces down the fence line. "Whoa, boy." He knew he ought to stop completely and let them both settle down a little. By now Czar's tail was raised like a flag, and when he looked back at Jesse the white showed in the corner of his eye. Crazy horse. What was he getting excited about? And why did he have to choose this morning for his performance?

"Whoa, Czar. Whoa there, fella. Easy. Easy." He did stop, only a few feet away, and extended his hand. "Whoa, Czar. Whoa, old fella." He stepped closer. Czar moved his head away, his eye on Jesse as though he were a stranger. "Whatsa matter, Czar old fella? You tryin' to kid me? Settle down, now. We got no time to fool around this morning. Easy. Easy." His hand was inches from Czar's head. This was the time for the greatest caution. Czar backed off a step, then another. Jesse's chance was slipping away. He lunged, and slipped the bridle rein around the horse's neck, but his sudden movement startled Czar, who jerked away. Jesse clung on, stumbling after him, causing the horse to sidestep nervously. If only Jesse could get his feet under him—but Czar moved just fast enough to keep Jesse's boots half dragging in the grass. As though he were shying from some lurching monster, Czar threw up his head and reared. The bridle rein pulled free. The big bay turned, galloped to the far end of the pasture, and stopped close beside the stable door. Jesse ran after him, turning just far enough out of his path to pick up the shotgun. He didn't want to come back for it. If old Czar felt like a run, he could get his fill of it taking Jesse to catch the train. He'd have to travel flat out all the way if they made it now, and Jesse was determined to make it, even if that meant chasing the train halfway to Banner.

He had no watch, but he didn't need one to know he was out of time. From now on if he missed a single movement, he was finished. If he fumbled a latigo strap, it would cost him his ticket on the last train out of purgatory. He was breathing hard, whether from running or frustration, he wasn't sure. He kept running, all the same. Czar stood by the stable, head and tail high. At that moment Jesse heard hoofbeats coming up behind him, and Buster the pinto pony galloped by, snorting as though he were trying to imitate Czar. With his fat body and short legs, though, he only looked ridiculous. He galloped straight to Czar, switched his tail, turned, and started off again. Czar swung around to face Jesse. He seemed to be looking down his nose at him. Puny man. What do you think you're going to do? This was the final betrayal—his horse had joined the rest of the world against him. At that moment the second whistle blew—the departure whistle. They'd missed the train. Czar reared slightly, with neck bowed, then galloped straight at Jesse, as if he were playing a game.

But Jesse was not playing games. He dropped the bridle, took a shotgun shell from his jumper pocket, loaded, and fired at the horse's chest. Czar squealed. His front legs went from under him, and he rolled on the grass, where he lay, thumping his head on the ground, his hind legs kicking convulsively. He squealed each time he raised his head.

Jesse couldn't take his eyes off Czar, writhing, his front quarters speckled with blood. But even if he had possessed the power to turn his back, nothing could have blocked out the almost human cries of pain. They penetrated so deeply inside him that he felt he would carry them with him forever, that on earth or in hell he would never escape them. His vision of Czar blurred as his eyes filled with tears.

There was, in his life, one more necessary act. He tried to blur his mind, as his sight was blurred. Walking toward Czar, he wiped his shirt sleeve across his eyes, so for a moment he could see more clearly. Down the long scrolled barrel of the shotgun he saw Czar's face, only inches beyond, still raising itself, and then falling to the ground. As it raised again, Jesse pulled the trigger. The head fell back; the squealing stopped. Jesse looked away.

He sank to his knees on the cold grass. Then, as he looked down, he saw, still in his hands, the barrel of the shotgun, strangely warped and rippled through his tears. He rose to his feet, and taking the end of the cold barrel in his hands, he spun himself around and around, arms extended, and let the shotgun go in a twisting arc that raised it against the sky, then let it fall back to earth, hidden forever among the tufted grass. Hidden? Though he closed his eyes tight, Jesse could still see its ugly black length cartwheeling in the midst of a quiet blue morning.

Again he sank to the ground, his palms pressed against

[*6* 2]

his wet cheeks. He bent lower, until his forearms were on the ground. Then slowly he straightened his body. At last he lay full length in the cold, damp grass. He wanted to go and bathe his hands in Czar's warm blood, then never wash it off, so that wherever he went in the world, the people he met would know what he had done. The air about him seemed absolutely still. As he lay there, the warmth of the sun gradually penetrated the back of his shirt, as if to compensate for the cold that was slowly freezing him from beneath. He shrank from the sun. It seemed to extend a forgiveness of which he was not worthy, while the earth, a closer witness, remained cold and silent, with a vast, oppressive stillness that forcefully testified to his wickedness. He waited for his punishment. He longed for it. Far off, he heard the train whistle again. Then the silence returned. At last he realized that his punishment was simply to go on without absolution—to carry the weight of what he had done to the end of whatever road this was that he was cursed to travel.

CHAPTER IX

GRADUALLY the sun moved higher, drying the field around him. He knew he would soon have to rise. The hardest thing to accept would be the body of Czar, stretched on the ground beside him. In a few days it would begin to swell, the upper legs would rise like accusing fingers pointed at Jesse. When the Indian dogs found the carcass, they would snarl and fight over it for days, tearing the hide and stripping the bones; birds would peck out the eyes; worms would thrive in the rotting flesh, until all that was left would be a bleached skeleton, with empty eye sockets and grinning teeth, small tatters of horsehide clinging to the jaw and shoulder bones. They'd have to be moving on. Jesse could not live with that hourly reminder of his crime.

He heard running footsteps. His first impulse was to jump up and smile as if he had just been having a rest, but he knew that would only make him look more ridiculous. A short way from him the running stopped, and he could hear quick, youthful puffing. One of the boys. Jesse couldn't face Ethan again. Not now. While he lay there wondering what to do, there were more footsteps. They stopped beside the first, and their sound was also replaced by anguished puffing. Jesse waited.

At last George found enough breath to speak. "Is he dead?"

"I don't know," Ethan said. "Czar sure is."

"He is?" George asked.

"Look at him—his whole face blown in."

When George spoke again he had moved to one side, where he must have gone to inspect Czar. "Ooh, yah," he said, with a shiver in his voice. Jesse heard him moving around, and looking through his fingers saw the little boy squat on his heels, with his head cocked to one side, looking at his father.

Ethan said, "Can you see anything?"

"He's dead," George replied.

"He couldn't be."

"He ain't moving." George thrust both fists into his eyes and began to cry. "He's dead."

Ethan came around then and stood beside his brother. Jesse tried to hold his breath. There would be advantages in having them think he was dead. When they went for help, he would have a chance to slip away. "There isn't any

[*64*]

blood," Ethan said. "Maybe Czar kicked him in the head. Maybe he's just knocked out."

"He's dead," George repeated, sniffling. "I know he's dead."

"Touch him," Ethan said.

"Touch him? What for?"

"To see if he's dead. Touch his skin, and if it's cold, that means he's dead."

"You touch him. I don't want to touch him."

"What's the matter? Scared?"

"No. I ain't scared."

"Then touch him."

"I ain't goin' to touch a dead man."

Through the crack in his fingers Jesse could see Ethan's boots approach him, but the boy's face was out of his range of vision. Jesse closed his eyes. For a moment he stopped breathing. He felt Ethan's fingers touch the back of his hand. Then Ethan said, "He's cold."

"See, I told you," George said.

"But there isn't any hole in him."

"He's dead," George repeated. Then, still sobbing, he said angrily, "The old bugger. What did he have to go and die for, anyway?"

"Why shouldn't he die, if he wants to?" Ethan said.

"I'm an orphan," George said, "I'm too small to be an orphan."

"You're not an orphan," Ethan told him. "Not while Mama's still alive."

"Will we go to live with Mama now?"

"Not as long as she stays with Keno."

"Then what'll happen to us?"

"We'll be all right. We can take care of ourselves."

[*6 5*]

After a pause, Ethan said, "You stay here with him while I get Buster."

"I'll come with you," George said.

"We shouldn't leave him. A hawk might come and peck out his eyes."

"We'll be right back."

"No. One of us has to stay with him. Would you rather get Buster?"

"What do you want Buster for, anyway?"

"He's too big for us. Buster'll have to drag him over to the grave."

"You going to bury him? Like you said?"

"If I don't, we'll have to tell the neighbors, and then Mama will come for us."

"I want Mama to come for us."

"And take us to live with Keno?"

"I don't care."

"You stay here. I'll get Buster."

"I'm scared, Ethan."

"I'll be right back." Ethan walked away.

George still sat on his haunches. When he turned his head to look at Jesse again, his face was pale and his eyes wide. He had quit crying. Jesse had better do something fast or these gravediggers would have him six feet under. He stirred slightly, and groaned.

George sprang to his feet and began to back away. "Oooo," he sobbed. Then he yelled, "Ethan!"

Jesse raised himself slightly. "I'm all right, George," he said.

"Ethan!" George screamed. He turned to run, glanced back at Jesse once, then ran after his brother, skimming over the meadow like a low-flying bird. "Eth-a-a-a-n!"

Jesse sat up. Ethan had not yet made it to the stable

when he heard George's cries, and turned around. They met in the pasture, and then came back toward Jesse, with George walking behind, peeking around Ethan's legs. Jesse stared back at them as they approached. Nobody spoke until the boys stopped in front of him.

"We were afraid you were dead," Ethan said. "What happened?"

Jesse shrugged. "Old Czar went crazy, I guess. I had to shoot him or he'd have got me sure."

"You're not dead!" George cried. He came from behind Ethan and ran to Jesse, his arms closing tight around his neck.

"No, I'm not dead." Jesse hugged the little body against him.

Ethan stood looking down; then suddenly plunged forward, stumbling to his knees, and threw his arms around both of them. "Oh, Jesse," he sobbed. "I was so scared."

CHAPTER X

IT was then, in that moment when he felt closer to his boys than he ever had, that Jesse suddenly realized that he must send them away. The realization brought a pang —not so much that he was losing them, as that he had failed them. He had tried—the good Lord knew he had tried—but nothing seemed to work. Their situation only seemed to get worse, and he felt in his bones that he had neither the strength nor will nor understanding to make it better. It was not fair to endanger the boys' future by persisting.

He pushed George off his lap and stood up. "Boys," he said. "There's something I want to tell you. You're going to live with your mama."

The moment of closeness had passed. Ethan flinched as though Jesse had struck him. "We can't," he said. "She doesn't even want us."

"Of course she wants you. It wasn't you she ran away from, it was me. And she did right, too. Only she should have taken you with her."

"You've been kicked in the head," Ethan told him.

"No, I haven't. I'll write your mama and tell her you're coming on the train. And you're going to go, so don't give me any more talk."

"I'll get off the first time the train stops. I'm not going to live with Keno."

"That's fine. You do as you please, so long as I don't know about it." Jesse started walking toward the house, conscious of his sons watching him. He raised his head, squared his shoulders, and marched across the meadow away from his boys.

When he got to the house he emptied his pockets of his hastily packed possessions. If the boys were going, he might as well stay here. And they were going whether they liked it or not. He was surprised he hadn't thought of this solution long ago. They'd be a lot better off with Shirley, and Jesse could somehow make his adjustment to life if he didn't have these kids forever on his mind—wondering what they'd eat, and what they'd wear, and what they must think of their father. If they caught the train a week from Thursday, that would give his letter time to reach Shirley so she could meet them.

He returned the little framed picture of her to the tray in the bedroom. A man with any gumption would have tossed it out the window. Jesse never looked at it any more. If by chance he did, the old yearning came back as strong as ever, and so the small gold frame had become an invisible point of uncommon power, like a pole where all the meridians of his life came together. Without it he was afraid he would lose any sense of direction.

There was a pencil among the other things on the tray. Jesse picked it up and sharpened it with his pocketknife. The shavings fell on the floor. He realized that he didn't have any paper in the house. Sometimes he wrote letters on the back of a calendar pad, but there was not even a calendar in this spare little house. The only book he owned was a Bible he had carried since his wedding day. He opened it and read again the inscription he had made on the ornamental title page: "Jesse and Shirley Gifford." He recalled the young man who had written those words as he might think of an old friend—someone he knew well but hadn't seen for years. What had ever become of him?

At the back of the Bible there were two or three blank pages. Jesse scored the inner edge of one with the blade of his knife and carefully tore it out. It didn't make a very big page to write on, but then he didn't have much to say. He cleared the kitchen table, brushed the crumbs onto the floor, and sat down with the piece of paper on the table in front of him, the pencil in his hand.

Dear Shirley.

That must be the right way to begin. It was important to keep this letter businesslike.

The boys are coming on the train and they should get in Calgary about a week from Friday. Keno's ranch was a long ways out of Calgary, but a hundred miles was nothing in that McLaughlin Buick. *Maybe you can check at the station and see what time the Lethbridge train gets in.*

Should he give some explanation? No. Ethan could explain when he got there, if he wanted to. Sign the letter and send it off. It said all that was needed just the way it was. He wrote his name at the bottom.

Jesse.

And he knew it wouldn't do. Somewhere he had to put in something with an edge to it. Deep under the scars of all her disappointments, Shirley still had soft, living tissue that would flinch if he could touch it. He turned the pencil upside down, and rubbed out the word *Jesse.* But what would he say? *I hope you are happy?* He hoped she was miserable.

We have a little house on the Belly River. It's not bad, but it needs a woman's hand.

He read what he had written. He erased it. Needs a woman's hand!

He brought the little gold frame from the bedroom, set it on the table in front of him, and looked at her. He shouldn't blame Keno. If things had been reversed, he'd have done the same thing. He didn't know how much she had been running to Keno, and how much she had been running away from Jesse. Perhaps if that itinerant photographer had come by about then, she would have gone with him instead of Keno. But that dumb photographer had come ten years too soon, with his Model T Ford and his camera and lights, driving up and down the lonely hills along the Red Deer River, taking pictures of cowboys and kids and ranchers' wives and prize bulls, and selling them back; taking pictures of Shirley and her baby. He didn't charge her for the pictures—he would use them for advertising, he said. And when he found her name was Shirley Gifford, he knew her husband was Jesse Gifford the bronc rider, who would be coming home to lunch any minute.

So he went away. But he delivered the pictures during the Calgary Stampede, when he knew Jesse would be gone and Shirley would be alone at the cow camp with her new little baby. He must have driven a hundred and fifty miles through ruts and mud with one thing on his mind, because he could have simply mailed the pictures; a hundred and fifty miles through ruts and mud with the vision of a dark-haired angel luring him on; and a hundred and fifty miles home again all scratched and bruised, scarcely able to see through his swollen eye, and his groin burning with a different kind of fire kindled by a well-placed kick with her knee.

It had happened a couple of days before Jesse got home, and still Shirley greeted him with tears and trembling and a hunger for his body that he had never experienced before. And in the middle of the night she told him about the photographer, and the recollection of it made her cry again. She thought she had killed him with the iron frying pan, and she had saddled a horse and ridden for help, with Ethan on one arm. But when they got back the man was gone. He'd left the pictures, and a little spot of blood on the floor where his head had lain. And Jesse had hugged his virtuous, devilish, beautiful little wife to him, and marveled that such an exquisite property should belong to him. The next morning he would have gone after the photographer, but Shirley cried and wouldn't let him leave her. After that, whenever he went stampeding he took Shirley and Ethan with him, or when George was a baby he left them at the main ranchhouse, or with friends.

In some ways Jesse was indebted to that man with his camera. Shirley had been a different woman afterward—more grown-up and exciting. And without that man, Jesse would not have this picture to torment and delight him.

He looked again at the piece of paper in front of him.

Wasn't there something in her life so personal that she wouldn't explain it to Keno, even if she did let him read it? Something that Jesse knew only the two of them could share? Looking at the picture of his wife, he remembered the day he married her. Then he wrote the single word *Goldenrod.* That was what he had been looking for. He signed his name at the bottom again, *Jesse.* When he got to Lone Rock he could buy an envelope and stamp. He lay back on his bunk to wait for the boys to come home.

CHAPTER XI

ABOUT noon George wandered back to the house.

"Where's Ethan?" Jesse asked.

"Gone."

"Gone where?"

"Gone. Run away. He says he's not coming back." George sat solemnly on a kitchen chair, swinging his bare feet, while Jesse fixed some lunch for them. Then he pulled his chair up to the table and ate his sandwich, his head tipped far back while he chewed, his eyes on the ceiling. Through the afternoon the two of them inhabited the cabin, but George acted as if he were completely alone. He did not speak or look at his father, and when Jesse spoke to him he pretended not to hear. The sun went down, and they got in their beds, and presently Jesse could hear George crying.

"Ethan'll be all right," Jesse said. "He knows how to take care of himself."

The quiet sobs and sniffles continued.

"If it was some kids, you'd worry," Jesse went on, "but not Ethan. He may be out there all alone in the dark somewhere, but he's not worried—not for a minute. Like as not he figured out a way to cook some supper, and right now he's fast asleep in a haystack somewhere. You don't have to worry about him."

The sound of crying subsided. George sniffled, and wiped his eyes with the blanket. Jesse could see his small pale face staring at the ceiling. "Why didn't he take me with him?" George asked.

Jesse felt like a jailer. Perhaps he lacked the skill, but he had the instinct. He would hang on to George as long as he could. If he had been able, he'd still have Ethan locked in his jail. Yes, and Shirley too, no matter how she cried to get away.

Several times during the day he had almost started after Ethan, to bring him back. For all his brave words, he was sick at the thought of the boy spending the night alone on the prairie. But there was something indefinable involved: something nebulous, yet very real. His son's dignity required that his decision to leave them be honored. Jesse could not bring himself to risk wounding that boyish pride. He told himself, as he told George, that Ethan would be all right.

His room was gray—bare walls as flat and blank as concrete, and on the wall opposite the window a square of moonlight was crossed by pane dividers as black as iron bars. It might have been a cell, and Jesse himself the prisoner.

Outside in the darkness he heard hoofbeats coming down the hill—quick, short steps of small hooves landing in the dust. At first the sound was so faint that it might have been no more than an illusion, as if the night could create images of sound as well as vision. But soon the hoofbeats were unmistakably clear, passing down the road by his window.

A few minutes later, when he heard boots coming quickly up the path and into the kitchen, Jesse raised himself on his elbow. "Ethan?"

"You awake, Jesse?" The boy appeared in the doorway. "I was afraid you'd be asleep, and I didn't know whether to wake you or not."

"I'm awake."

Ethan sat on the bunk opposite, in the light from the window. "You'll never guess what I found." He scarcely paused. "A ranch. The prettiest little ranch you ever did see. Right in the foothills. A creek running through it. And plenty of shelter for the stock. There's a house, and a barn, and a hay shed. Some machinery, but of course I don't know whether that goes or not."

"You mean it's for sale?"

"What?"

"The ranch is for sale?"

"Sure it is. There's a sign nailed to the fence post along the road. *Ranch for Sale.* Man. Those old mountains lean right over top of it, like as if they wouldn't let a hailstone hit it, nor a scrap of wind pull at it. Just like it was locked tight in a closet full of sunshine . . ."

"How big is it?"

"What?"

"How many acres?"

"Well, it can't be too big, 'cause there's just an old log house. It's nice, set down under the trees by the creek, but it looks like no more'n three or four rooms. A big spread would have a better house than that."

"Then you don't know the price, either."

"The sign didn't say, and I didn't talk to anybody, of

course. Just rode in and looked at it from on top of the hill. There was a woman and a couple of girls out in the yard sometimes, but I didn't see anybody else. I just sat there on that hill all afternoon, and the longer I sat, the more at home I felt. Jesse, don't you reckon we could buy that ranch?"

"I couldn't buy the sweat off a sick bull, and you know it."

"You could if you went back to riding."

Jesse sighed. How simple the world is when you are young. You wanted a ranch, you entered the saddle-bronc contest, and with your winnings you bought a ranch. It was not strange that Ethan should have this vision—he had been raised on it. But wasn't it time now that he began to face reality? He was twelve years old. Twelve? Hah! Jesse had carried that dream till he was almost thirty. "It's late," he said. "You'd better get to sleep."

"I can't sleep," Ethan replied, and walked to the doorway. "You can do it, Jesse. I know you can." He returned to the bed and sat down again. "Just say it has two hundred acres. Just say it, okay?"

"Okay." Immediately Jesse wished he had withheld even that much encouragement.

"Two hundred acres. Say five dollars an acre. There wasn't any crop land. Only hay and pasture—and trees. And creek. Jesse. I wish you could have seen it. Say five dollars an acre. That's a thousand dollars. Man. You could win that much easy."

Jesse had let this go on for too long. "Maybe if I was ten years younger," he said. "And if I had better luck than I did ten years ago. Then maybe I could win a thousand dollars."

"But you can try . . ."

[*75*]

"Listen to me. Suppose it's five hundred acres instead of two. Suppose it's ten dollars an acre instead of five. That's five thousand dollars. Where you going to win that kind of money?"

"But you don't know . . ."

"And that's just the bare land. What good's the land going to do you if you don't have any cattle to run on it? And where you going to get the cattle?"

"There were cattle on the place. Maybe they're for sale, too."

"You've still got to pay for them. And how you going to run cattle without a few head of horses? What about machinery to cut your hay? Where are you going to get harnesses, shovels, tools, wire to mend your fence? A wagon? Do you think that stuff grows on trees? But what are we talking for? I can't ride broncs any more, anyway."

"I'll bet you can ride 'em good as ever."

"No, I can't."

"How do you know you can't?"

"I tried."

"Go on. You have not."

"The other day. When I went to Macleod with J. T."

"You did?"

"We were sitting in the beer parlor, and decided to go to the Stavely Stampede. And I tried to ride a bronc."

"Why didn't you tell us?"

"A dirty old plowhorse. He flang me thirty feet high."

"You were drunk."

"That doesn't matter."

"It does matter. You can't ride a rocking horse when you're drunk. That's what Mama used to say."

"How'd you remember that?"

"I remember."

"It doesn't matter. I'm through riding broncs. Keno can do that from now on."

"And what are you going to do?"

"As I damn please."

Ethan pulled off his boots and threw them into a corner.

"You might just as well forget about it," Jesse went on, feeling strangely cruel and powerful. "In the first place, I'm not riding any bucking horses. And if by any chance I won a pot of money, do you think I want to spend the rest of my days grubbing on some two-bit spread, trying to keep from starving to death?"

"Yes," Ethan said. "Yes, I do." The words fell across Jesse's mind like a gate; suddenly he could think of nothing more to say. Ethan pulled off his shirt and overalls, and slipped into bed beside his brother. After a while he said, "I wish I hadn't come back."

CHAPTER XII

AFTER breakfast the next morning Jesse sent the boys to borrow a horse from J. T. so he could ride up to Lone Rock and mail his letter. He was still busy trying to straighten the house when he heard Ethan call. The shouts were coming from down by the barn. He took the letter from his shirt pocket and read it through once more as he walked down the path to the stable. There he found the boys, George still on the pinto and Ethan standing near by, holding the bridle of a big brown gelding, all saddled and ready to go.

"J. T. says you can borrow Zigzag for a day or two,"

Ethan said. "Says maybe you can ride him a little and wear down that hump in his backbone."

It looked as if J. T. had figured out a way to get Jesse to break his broncs without having to pay for it. Well, Jesse needed a horse; he wasn't fussy about what kind. He took the bridle reins from Ethan. "I'll be back this afternoon," he said. "I'm just going to mail a letter to your mama. You fellows will be catching the train a week from Thursday morning, so you might as well settle yourselves to it."

With his left foot in the stirrup, and his right hand on the saddle horn, he raised himself to the horse's back. He could feel its muscles under the saddle as hard and square as a stack of lumber. He touched his spurs to the gelding's sides. Zigzag did not step forward, but arched his back and crow-hopped. As he lowered his head, Jesse pulled on the bridle reins, which seemed to come loose in his hand. He saw that one cheekstrap on the bridle was unfastened, and the throat latch was not buckled. When Zigzag's head went down, the bit slipped out of his mouth and the whole bridle came off back over his ears. Jesse glanced at Ethan, who was standing with a broad grin on his face. "Ride 'im, cowboy!" Ethan yelled.

The little devil. He had set this up. Jesse's impulse was to get down and whip him, but it was too late. Zigzag came up under him. The bridle trailed from Jesse's hand like an empty basket. He tossed it away.

"Ride 'im, Jesse!" George's shrill young voice shouted.

Ride 'im. Hah! The little rascals had gotten him into this, and he'd get out of it any way he could. He made a grab for the saddle horn, but stopped his hand just short of it. He felt just enough sand in his craw for one more challenge. He took the jolt of landing with both hands free, and as they started up again, his spurs were sunk in Zigzag's shoulders.

[*78*]

"Wa-hoo!" he yelled. Might as well give the boys their money's worth. He leaned back in the saddle, trying to make his body flow to the motion of the horse's plunging leaps.

There was no horn, or pickup men, or catchpen. He and Zigzag were cut loose in time and space, with no restrictions on either. But he felt good. The old blister knew how to buck, and to stay aboard him Jesse would have to know how to ride. Zigzag bucked straight across the pasture, then along the fence so close that once he lunged against it, causing the wires to screech. Jesse bent his leg, and the barbs tore Zigzag's side instead of his rider's calf. With a groan of pain, or perhaps rage or frustration, the horse turned back toward the middle of the pasture, seeming to leap higher and harder with every jump. The two boys ran behind and mingled their cheers with Zigzag's thumping snorts. The rascals! How did they know Zigzag wouldn't kill their father? But Jesse had to admit that Ethan was right about one thing—he could ride a lot better when he was sober.

In one of his turning plunges, Zigzag suddenly came upon Czar's body, still bright in the sun, his eyes staring, as though he had lain down to ease the pain from the hole in his head. Zigzag squealed at the sight of him, and whirled away with a sudden burst of new vigor. It did not last long. Each lunge required greater effort, and at the end of one he stopped completely. Jesse spurred him. He crow-hopped a few more jumps and stopped again, head down, breathing heavily. He only winced when Jesse raked him with the spurs. Though he had worked himself into a good sweat, he was far from exhausted; he was just too canny to continue when he knew he had been licked.

Ethan ran up. "See what I told you, Jesse. You can ride as good as ever." He was holding Jesse's shotgun in his hand.

"Where'd you get that?"

"I found it—over there in the grass. Don't you want it any more?"

"Of course I do."

George came cavorting behind, mimicking with his childish leaps the futile efforts of Zigzag. "Wa-hoo!" George cried. "Ride 'im, cowboy." He sprawled in the grass, then was up and bucking again.

Jesse swung down from the saddle. "Where's that bridle? Maybe now Zigzag is ready for a jog up town."

"You don't have to mail that letter now," Ethan said. "George and I can stay here."

"What do you mean?" Jesse asked him.

"That wasn't just a joke," Ethan said. "That was to show you that you can still ride broncos. I asked J. T. if he had a horse that liked to buck, and he said he sure did."

"So I can ride that spavined old plowhorse. What does that prove?"

"It proves that you're still the champ."

"I never was the champ."

"All right. You could be."

"I'm too old," Jesse said.

He saw J. T. coming across the pasture toward him. "You're some rider after all, Jesse. Ain't many cowboys can stick old Zigzag when he gets going."

"He does have a mighty rough gallop."

"What say you and me be partners after all?"

"No sir. I'm not breaking my neck for anybody."

"What's the matter? Is it the fifty-percent split? Don't worry about it. I'll give you seventy-five."

"You're generous with my prize money, J. T. If there is any, I'll give you ten percent."

They finally settled on a twenty-eighty split. Jesse took the letter out of his pocket and tore it in little pieces, letting them flutter from his hands onto the grass.

ON the day of the Macleod Stampede, he found himself with the other cowboys waiting to register for the saddle-bronc event. Keno was there, standing in front of the chutes and looking at Jesse as though he were a receptacle for spit. "Hello, Jesse," he said.

"Hello." Jesse's whole rib cage seemed to collapse inside him—not because of Keno, but because he knew if Keno was there, Shirley would not be far away.

"That's Keno," Ethan muttered beside him.

And George, coming along behind, cried, "Where? Where?"

Jesse hurried the boys away from the chutes. "Yes. That's Keno," he said. What had possessed him? By what obscure reasoning had he convinced himself that he could compete again? Here he was, old and broken, going up against Keno and a flock of younger cowboys eager to win their spurs. The ride on Zigzag had started it, of course. After that there had been further thoughts of the Gillespie ranch—crawl back to San Soucie, take up his place beside Lars, and wait to die. God. That could take forty years.

Then, too, he had changed after the ride on Zigzag. He had felt a new man grow inside him—start in the middle and grow outward, replacing the old Jesse as stone replaces rotten wood in a petrified tree; a man too good for San Soucie's jibes—a man perhaps even capable of achieving the old dream.

Jesse scanned the distant faces in the bleachers—all

tiny blurs, indistinguishable from so far away—until he saw Shirley. She had a yellow ribbon in her hair.

Ethan saw him staring at the crowd. "Is Mama here?" he asked.

"She's here," Jesse replied. "Right over there in the bleachers."

"Let's go see her."

"You boys go ahead."

"What about you?"

"The show's about ready to start. I better stay here. Just tell her hello for me, will you?" He watched the boys hurry away. Tell her hello for Jesse. And when she says, "Who's Jesse?" tell her he's that spavined old cowboy she used to love, back when she was just a girl. She'll remember. No matter what has happened since, she still gave her first pure love to that cowboy. And for years after, that love had grown. It wasn't what he'd done, but what he hadn't been able to do, that killed it. If he had been champion, and bought a ranch, how different it could have been. She wasn't made to live in a shack out on Gillespie's, with no hope for anything more as long as she lived.

And now he realized that the circumstances had not changed her until they changed him. As long as he worked for something, she stayed. But when he gave up, when he accepted his defeat and began pushing a broom in rhythm with old Lars, she couldn't stand it. For the first time he understood what she had been trying to say when she pleaded with him to leave Gillespie's.

They were lying side by side, naked in bed. Their lovemaking had become a ritual, its form maintained for tradition's sake, its meaning lost. And Jesse felt a sort of terror grip him. Was this what happened after you had been married for only nine years? Could the furnace cool so quickly?

[*82*]

"Jesse," Shirley said. In the moonlight he could see her face on the pillow, her dark hair piled in disarray where his hands had so recently entangled it. She turned toward him, and with her hand she reached across and touched his cheek. "Jesse."

He waited for her to say more, but she didn't speak again, and as he watched, her eyes filled with tears. Oh God. Was this the way love dies? "It'll be all right," he said.

"It won't be all right. Not as long as we stay here."

"Here at Gillespie's. They took me on when I was just out of the hospital. Our money was gone—I had to have a job, didn't I?"

"Then you had to, yes."

"And I need one now. I can't go back to riding yet."

"It's been a year and a half." She never seemed to believe that his back still hurt. She wanted him to return to the arena and start making money.

"I can't help it. My back still isn't better. I've got to wait."

"Then let's go somewhere else to wait."

"I can't walk out on San Soucie, just when I get well enough to be some use to him."

"Then tell him to pay you full wages."

"He paid me part wages when I wasn't good for anything. I can't talk about more money yet."

She took her hand away from contact with him, and pressed the back of it against her mouth. He could see the sobs move up her throat, only to be stifled by that firm, determined hand. Presently she said, "Can't you see what's happening? San Soucie hopes you never do get better. He likes to have a champion for a chore boy. It puts brine in his belly to yell at you and have you do what he says."

[*83*]

"San Soucie has been good to us," he insisted. "We ought to be grateful."

"Well, I'm sorry if I'm not what I ought to be," Shirley said. "But I'm not grateful."

At last Jesse understood. Three years too late he saw that she had been trying to save the old Jesse—the one she loved. Now the new Jesse, old beyond telling, must enter the arena and have her watch his humiliation.

The afternoon's events began. And though Jesse competed, though he was caught in the dust and whirl and noise of the stampede, he moved through the day like a tin soldier, head erect, eyes straight ahead, lips fixed, expression never changing. Finally, somehow, his ordeal was over, and they were in the Dodge driving back over the humps of the Blue Trail toward home. George's cheeks were still flushed from the touch of his mother's lips as he told about Shirley, and how she bought him popcorn, and hot dogs, and ice cream and sodas. Ethan said she had asked about Jesse, and wanted to see him. Ethan had taken the first prize in the boys' steer riding, and had ten dollars in his pocket to prove it.

J. T. smiled in the driver's seat, and talked about the future of their partnership. Jesse, too, had winnings in his pocket, but he wasn't even sure how much. All he knew was that Shirley had been in the stands, and watched him win. He was still a tin soldier, staring straight ahead, his body as hard as petrified rock. He saw clearly the central truth of the day's events: she had watched him win. For all the money in his pocket, he knew that Shirley was the prize, and though Keno took her home with him tonight, the competition had only begun.

CHAPTER XIII

IT rained in the night. Covered by the darkness, heavy clouds rolled in on their rumbling wheels, and for an hour or so Jesse was kept halfway between sleeping and waking by the drone of water on the roof. By morning the storm had passed. The clouds moved steadily eastward, and above them the light came up in a blue sky. The boys were still asleep. Yesterday had been a big day for them, especially Ethan. He had tasted blood as a competing cowboy, and no one knew better than Jesse the powerful effect of that first sip. Half proudly, half with a sinking heart, Jesse acknowledged to himself that there was another bronc-buster in the family.

He heard a tractor coming down the road outside his window, and sat up. It was J. T. Jones. He stopped outside the door, and leaving the tractor to idle, came up the path. Jesse grabbed his overalls, and pulled them on as he stood up. He felt the roll of bills in his pocket. He'd forgotten about that. This called for some sort of celebration. School was out, Jesse and Ethan had both won at the stampede, and they had some money. Tomorrow, the first of July, they'd be off to Raymond for the stampede, so maybe it would be better to celebrate today by rambling down the river. They might even snare some fish. He hurried out to meet J. T. at the kitchen door, his fingers across his lips. "The kids are still asleep."

"Well, get 'em up," J. T. said. "We've got work to do today."

"You can't hay today. It's too wet."

"There's more things in the world than hay. My old sheepherder's half crazy with pain. I got to get him to a dentist, so I reckon you and the boys will have to mind the sheep."

Sheep! Mind the sheep? Was J. T. crazy? Jesse restrained himself. For a while, at least, he must humor that man. Though he had a little money in his pocket now, he still needed J. T. badly. He didn't even have a horse any more to get him to Raymond for the next stampede. "I'm not a sheepherder, J. T. I'm a cowboy."

"Today you're a sheepherder. Besides, you know a cowboy is only a sheepherder with his brains knocked out. I'm giving you a promotion." He added, "If I only get twenty percent of your winnings, you'll have to work like a Tartar in between stampedes to pay your way."

Jesse sighed. J. T. was just a carbon copy of San Soucie —a little fainter, but he said the same thing: I've got you where I want you, Jesse Gifford. You can squeal all you want, but I've got you by the short hairs and you're going to do as I say.

"We'll be over after breakfast," Jesse said.

J. T. was halfway to his tractor when he turned and called, pushing the knife a little deeper into Jesse, "Say, Jesse. I thought I'd drag your dead horse away." He flicked his thumb in the direction of the pasture. "He'll make good pig feed."

As soon as breakfast was ready, Jesse called the boys. Ethan was up at once, sitting at the table with a faraway look in his eyes. It was a few minutes later before George came in from the bedroom, swaying unsteadily and walking from side to side. Jesse should have let him sleep. They ate almost in silence. George was too sleepy to talk, Ethan's mind was on his own private dreams, and Jesse was trying to form

[*8 6*]

in his mind the proper words to express what he had to say.
At last he remarked, "J. T. was over this morning. He wants
us to herd his sheep today."

Ethan's dark eyes turned toward Jesse as if he did not
understand. "He what?"

"His old herder has a tooth that's killing him. Has to
take him to the dentist. So today we're sheepherders."

"Not me," Ethan said. He drew himself up to indicate
by the square of his shoulders an attitude suitable to a
future world's champion.

"Yes, you," Jesse said. "That is, if you want to go to the
stampede tomorrow."

"Are you sick, Jesse?" Ethan exclaimed.

"No. Just that if we expect J. T. to tote us around and
pay us wages, we have to lend a hand in between."

"I never expected to see the day," Ethan said.

"It won't kill you," Jesse said. "You can bring Buster
if you want to."

Jesse walked over to J. T.'s, with Ethan and George
riding beside him on the pinto. When they got there the old
herder was already in the car, his bearded face framed by
the red bandana tied around his jaw. He was scarcely tall
enough to see out the window. A small black dog sat beside
the car, looking at her master.

J. T. hurried out of the house. "Oh, there you are." He
opened the car door, then turned to talk to Jesse. "You'll
have to hurry. I turned the sheep out a half an hour ago. Just
hold them on that river bottom." He waved his arm. "Keep
them out of the summerfallow on top of the hill or they'll
trample all the feed into the mud." He got in his car and
shut the door. As he turned the car around, he rolled down
the window. "And don't let them in the alfalfa. It's fenced,
but I got some breechy old ewes that'll try to get under or

over if you give them a chance. Just keep them a mile away from the alfalfa."

The sheepherder's dog stood beside the car, whining. "You won't be able to use that little bitch. She doesn't pay attention to anybody but Carl." The Dodge drove away, slewing a little as the tires slipped on the packed mud of the road through the barnyard. The dog ran behind.

"Well, boys," Jesse said. "Let's go find these sheep."

As soon as they caught up with the herd, Jesse realized that he had worried unnecessarily. Besides his revulsion for the animals, he had felt hesitant to accept the responsibility for creatures as ornery as sheep were reputed to be. He hadn't the faintest notion what sheepherding consisted of, but as they came through the trees and he saw the quiet tableau of the sheep grazing on the hillside, Jesse felt a sort of peace come over him. Really, this could be a very pleasant day. The world was so clean after the rain, and now the sun grew warm on his shirt. They climbed to the top of the hill, where they could have a good view of the pasture land beneath them, and stretching off to the north the almost level field of summerfallow, green with stinkweeds, thistles, and wild oats. Far to the east, on the other side of the summerfallow, Jesse could see the alfalfa patch, emerald in color and tinged with the smoke of pale violet blossoms.

"Well," he said, as he sat down on a thick tuft of grass with his back against a fence post. "Looks like it'll be a tough day." Ethan stayed on Buster's back, but George slid off and came to sit by his father. "How about a game of mumble-peg?" Jesse asked. He raised himself so that he could reach into his pocket for his knife. "Should be easy today, in this soft ground." He opened the blade and flipped the knife a couple of times so it sank point-first into the turf.

"Can I be first?" George asked. He took the knife, but was uncertain what to do with it.

"Front-hand," Jesse reminded him. "Then back-hand, breaks, picks . . ."

George laid the knife on his palm, with the point extending over his fingers. He raised his hand sharply, and the knife flew off and landed on the handle.

"Let me show you," Ethan said. He got off his horse and knelt beside them. Swiftly he went through front-hand, back-hand, breaks, picks, wrist, elbow, shoulder. On the third finger of breaks he missed once, but without hesitation, repeated it successfully. When he missed on jump-the-fence, though, he passed the knife to Jesse. He always had trouble with that one, and didn't want to risk losing all the ground he'd made.

Jesse played left-handed to give George encouragement, and on breaks he missed one, repeated it, missed again, which lost him his turn and sent him back to the beginning. "Now flip it a little," he said, demonstrating before he passed the knife to George. George flipped it, so high that it wobbled around in the air and then came down point-first close beside Jesse's leg.

"I got it!" George cried.

"Yes, you got it, and you almost got me. You'd better move back a bit."

"I didn't hit you."

"No. And I don't want you to."

George moved away a little and tried his back-hand.

As they played, a few of the sheep grazed up the hillside toward them, cropping the grass with their busy teeth. The game of mumble-peg was so quiet and subdued that before long they were surrounded by grazing sheep. The long-faced animals worked at their morning meal with a lofty seriousness. Occasionally one of them, raising her head to chew, would look down her nose at the man and boys with steady indifference.

"They make me nervous," Ethan said at last.

"Chase them away, then," Jesse told him. "They're pretty close to the summerfallow, anyway."

No doubt Ethan's thought was simply to chase them down the hill, but he lunged at them so suddenly that before two or three of the closest could get away, he was pounding their backs with his fists. Almost instinctively, he seized a big ewe by the wool on her shoulders, and straddling her, took a wild, humping ride down the hill, starting an avalanche of sheep around him. At the bottom of the hill most of the sheep stopped, but Ethan rode on across the flat, his legs swinging out at the sides, until he disappeared into the trees. In a moment he came walking back toward Jesse and George. He waved his arm and shouted, "That was fun."

As the morning progressed, they moved up and down the brow of the hill, wherever the sheep grazed too near to the summerfallow. For a while Jesse even contemplated spending his old age as a sheepherder—you certainly couldn't ask for a softer job than this. If you had a dog, you wouldn't even have to move. Drive them out in the morning; drive them home at night.

At noon Ethan rode back to the house to make some sandwiches. It was while they were eating their lunch that a black-faced ewe grazing at the top of the hill led a small band across the road onto the summerfallow. Ethan jumped on Buster and galloped away to drive them out. But by the time he returned to finish his sandwich, they were back in again, in greater numbers than before. Jesse noticed that when Ethan drove them out the second time, the old black-faced ewe walked across the road and stood with head up, waiting. The old biddy.

Jesse picked up the lunch sack. "Let's go up there to eat our lunch," he said. So they walked to the place where the black-faced ewe still stood waiting. Let her wait. They could sit right here in front of her all afternoon. But as he sat down, Jesse looked behind him and saw a fresh invasion of the summerfallow, with some sheep trotting in their eagerness to reach the green young stinkweeds. He stood up and handed Ethan another sandwich. "You go and drive them out. George and I will stay and watch here."

Ethan galloped toward the swiftly growing flock that spread across the summerfallow. Where earlier the sheep had turned and run when Buster galloped up, now they scarcely noticed. As Ethan turned them back at one place, others moved deeper into the forbidden field. At last he got off his horse, and shouting furiously, began to pelt the sheep with clods of dirt. "You stay here," Jesse said to George. "Don't let any sheep across the road. I've got to go and help Ethan."

Together, with Jesse throwing clods of dirt and Ethan galloping up and down on Buster, they finally drove the reluctant sheep back across the road and chased them down the hill toward the river. They looked over to see that George had been overwhelmed by another invasion, and hurried to help him. At last they had driven all the sheep out of the summerfallow. Jesse was puffing. He had always hated sheep for no reason. It was satisfying to him now to be justified in his loathing.

Though Jesse was glad to stop and catch his breath, the sheep did not seem to need any respite. Instead of pausing to graze on the brown sod of the river hill, they struck out like race horses along the length of the flat, and prepared another assault on the summerfallow at a point further west. Jesse and the boys had to hurry to turn them back again.

The sun had shone throughout the day, and on the

road the hard-packed tracks were dry, but the earth of the field was still dark with moisture from the rain. Jesse was tempted to let the sheep go—the only thing at stake was a hundred and sixty acres of stinkweeds. He knew, though, that pasturing them there in the mud would result in more feed being trampled than eaten. Perhaps they'd better keep trying. Turned away again, the sheep struck a fast course back down the river toward the east. Jesse didn't say anything to the boys, but inwardly he laughed. What a wonderful way to spend his old age.

At least he refused to hurry any more. He'd work away at it, but he wasn't going to give himself a heart attack for the sake of a few zillion stinkweeds. He walked slowly down the road, with George on one side of him and Ethan riding Buster on the other. In fact, he walked slower and slower. If J. T. loved his damn sheep so much, it should make him happy to know that they were enjoying themselves. By simply letting the sheep get a few mouthfuls of weeds, Jesse could make the whole world happy; most of all himself. He refused to worry about it any more.

He sat down on the crest of the hill to have a smoke. In front of him, the river wound through its broad valley, looping around cottonwood groves, and in places rushing swiftly beneath high cutbanks. The world was, after all, a quiet, friendly place, and it did no good to fight against it. The thing to do was pace yourself to the rhythm of the earth —at this time of year the summer processional, luxuriant and unhurried, as though the next two months would last a thousand years. The sheep had obviously eaten all they wanted today. Their only interest now was in running, which certainly wouldn't do them any good. He'd take them back to the bedground and let them spend the hot afternoon in the shade of the trees.

"They're getting in down there," Ethan said, and galloped away.

Jesse rose. "Come on, George. Let's go give him a hand."

Still, he didn't hurry. Quite deliberately he walked back to where the sheep were again spreading over the summerfallow like locusts in the land of promise. It took a little longer, but without too much exertion they were able to get all the sheep back over the hill again. At least he thought it was all of them, until he looked further on down, and saw a single line of sheep hurrying up over the brow of the hill toward the alfalfa patch, and disappearing through a hole in the fence.

Instantly, Jesse's composure was gone. He ran toward the fence. "Stop 'em!" he called to Ethan, who rode ahead, shouting. The line of sheep stopped to look at him. The grass was high along the fence line, and it wasn't until he got there that Jesse could see inside the field where perhaps twenty or thirty sheep grazed, only their woolly backs visible in the thick hay.

He vaulted the fence. "Come on, boys," he cried. "We've got to get them out of here quick." He ran around the sheep, shouting. They turned and moved back toward the fence, but the hole in the wire operated like a valve that would let them in, but seemed to close so they couldn't get out. Anyway, they pretended not to be able to find it and began eating the alfalfa again. Jesse looked up and down the fence, but for as far as he could see, there was no gate.

Now what would he do? He rushed two or three of the sheep against the fence, caught one by the wool on its shoulders, lifted, and thrust it over the fence. "Catch 'em!" he cried to the boys. "Don't let 'em eat." Already they were starting to swell, so that they couldn't run very fast, and one by one he or Ethan caught them, he rode them to the fence, and lifted them over. Every time he did, Jesse felt his back cave in a little more. Before they were finished, the last few sheep were down, their bellies huge, the skin on the inside of their flanks stretched tight, their mouths open, and bubbles of froth building outside their lips.

Jesse looked helplessly about. It was possible to save bloated sheep by puncturing them, but you had to know the right place. He hesitated for fear of stabbing the poor brutes to death. On the other hand, they had gorged themselves on green alfalfa—the gas would blow them up like balloons. They were going to die, anyway. He took out his pocketknife, opened the small blade, and knelt beside one of the bloated sheep. If he tried one, and did it right, then perhaps he could save the rest. If he killed her, he would only be hastening her death by a few minutes. He picked a spot on her swollen belly, high on her side and a little ahead of her hipbone. Then he raised his arm, and on that spot, brought the knife down point-first with all his strength. The rush of air from her body seemed to lift his hand away. He must have got it right. He rose, and stood looking at her for a moment, trying to gauge the success of his operation. But as he stood there, Ethan said, "J. T. Jones is here."

Jesse glanced up. The Dodge had stopped just outside the fence, and J. T. was running from one sick animal to the next, swinging his knife with swift assurance. He didn't even stop to kneel beside each one, but bent from the hips, placed his little finger over the animal's hipbone, or as close to it as he could find on her grotesquely swollen body, spanned a certain distance toward her ribs with his thumb, plunged the knife through the tight-stretched skin, and hurried on to the next. The swollen woolly bodies slowly deflated, so that by the time he reached the last one, the first looked almost normal. Behind him, the old herder came along, lifting the sheep to their feet and pausing occasionally to give an arm signal to his dog, who was over a quarter of a mile away, quietly driving the main herd of sheep out of the summerfallow.

Among them, they finally got most of the sheep back through the hole in the fence, and mended it. Six, though, lay dead in the alfalfa patch. One by one, J. T. took their hind legs, Jesse took their front, they carried them to the edge of the field, and with a one, two, three, swung them over the fence. The bodies landed on the other side with a thump and a curious rolling motion forward, then back, which almost made them seem alive.

J. T. looked at Jesse. "Six dead," he said.

Jesse tried to form in his mind the words to explain what had happened, but he realized there was no excuse for it. He hated excuses, even when they were good ones.

J. T. looked at him. "Your back bothering you?"

"I couldn't drive them through the fence," Jesse said. "I had to lift them over."

"You take care of that back," J. T. told him. "You're on deck for tomorrow, you know."

"I know," Jesse said.

They skinned the dead sheep, threw the hides in the trunk of the Dodge, and drove away, leaving the carcasses against the fence for the dogs to fight over. Jesse was glad to get home and lie down on his bunk. He was surprised that J. T. hadn't cursed him out. It was a good thing he hadn't, though. At this point that was all Jesse needed to make him give up the whole business.

CHAPTER XIV

THE morning of July the first was bright and hot. Jesse rose with mixed feelings of excitement and despair. Day before yesterday he had won. Now, today, in Raymond, he would be expected to repeat his triumph. He remembered then the burden of being champion—with winning came the pressure to win again. And if you were at the top, every two-bit cowboy who could pay the entry fee was in there trying to knock you off. You were fair game, and if you lost, nobody cared.

But it was worth it. It was worth the risk of poverty, humiliation, and being a cripple for life, because when you did win, there was nothing like that sweet taste of triumph. He'd go if it killed him, and by the way his back felt, perhaps it would.

Shortly after breakfast, J. T. called to pick them up, and as they drove along, Jesse looked around at his silent companions. George sprawled on the back seat, not fully awake yet. Ethan sat forward, his head between J. T. and Jesse, staring down the road ahead of them with an intensity that seemed capable of carrying them on even if the car ran out of gas. J. T. sat slouched behind the wheel. He was so short that it seemed doubtful he could see the road ahead of him, but rather than defer to the difficulty by stretching, he appeared to deny that it existed, and sat even lower than necessary. Jesse wished that if he was flying blind, he wouldn't drive so fast.

"How's the back?" J. T. asked him.

"Cracked glass," Jesse replied. He was a fool, a silly old fool of a cowboy galloping after trophies that would make suitable goals for a twenty-year-old. The five thousand or so people gathered at Raymond today would probably have a good laugh to see Father Time himself out there on a bucking horse. But he didn't mind the laughs. He knew a stampede crowd spent its time on the edge between groans and laughter. In his time, he had inspired both—he could still hear the moan from the grandstand, even above Sundown's thumping fury, when the big bay horse came down on him —and of the two, he preferred the laughter.

It wasn't the laughing five thousand he cared about, anyway—it was the one, the hundred-and-five-pound woman. Would she be laughing? As he thought about it, he found himself growing tense as a green kid going into the arena for the first time. That was one thing he didn't need, to get nervous. And all the way to Raymond he sat there in J. T.'s Dodge, watching the distant prairie slowly pass, his whole attention focused on forgetting Shirley.

As soon as they got to the stampede grounds, the boys hurried away to find their mother. J. T. went with Jesse to register for the saddle-bronc competition.

The afternoon dribbled away. The great climax for which he had tried to prepare himself never came off. He got through his ride, but the pain in his back held him from spurring as he would otherwise have done, and when it was over, his greatest feeling was one of relief. The first prize money went to Keno. Jesse was happy to have placed fourth. At least that should keep them from laughing at him. Maybe not Shirley—she knew the way he used to ride, and she would be able to see how he hugged the saddle now, as if he were afraid. She'd think that after all these years since Sundown, he'd still not got his nerve back. But it wasn't fear of the ride, or of falling off; it was pain, and the fear of pain, that made him cling that way. She couldn't know that, and so she'd laugh. Maybe even if she knew about the pain, she'd laugh at it. Heaven knew she'd caused him enough of it in the last couple of years.

As Jesse and J. T. walked back toward the car, the boys came running toward them out of the crowd. Ethan had taken the boys' steer-riding event again, and Jesse congratulated him. The kid had a gift. If he could just keep his bones intact, he'd be riding in the big time some day, and for the life of him, Jesse could not make himself believe that it would be a bad fate.

Ethan walked up close to Jesse and whispered, "Mama wants to see you."

Why would Shirley want to see him? "You go ahead," Jesse said to J. T. and George. "We'll see you at the car."

"I want to come with you," George said.

"No. You go with Mr. Jones."

Jesse followed Ethan back through the crowd of people who were walking toward the gate, or to their cars. A few of them hurried; most walked slowly—even children seemed bemused, as if by simple concentration they could preserve for a few moments longer the excitement which the day had held.

But the spell was broken. The flag came down. The band members had put their instruments in heavy black cases and were leaving the grounds with the other people. Their red and gold uniforms, so grand when they were all together, now, seen by ones and twos, appeared tawdry and almost ludicrous. Underfoot, paper cups and hot-dog wrappers strewed the dusty ground. Ethan led his father to the front of the grandstand, and began mounting the broad stairway of seats that reached up into the shadows. The seats were empty now, gray and limitless beneath their gabled canopy. In the middle of them, as if placed there for effect, or scale comparison, sat one solitary figure. Jesse was amazed to think that anything so small could leave so great a cave of longing when it was gone. Ethan ran ahead of him, and reached her first. As Jesse approached them, they sat side by side looking at him.

Jesse stopped in front of her. "Hello," he said.

"Hello, Jesse." For a moment she looked directly into his eyes, then she turned back toward Ethan. He remembered when he saw her in profile that her lower lip was slightly indented under her teeth, which gave her a hint of a lisp. It seemed strange that he should forget that. He had thought he remembered all of her. "Your back hurts, doesn't it?" she asked. She still didn't look at him again.

"A little."

"I could tell the way you rode this afternoon."

"It's not bad now. Not like it was."

"And the way you climbed the stairs just now. I should have come to meet you, but I wanted to be away from people." She roughed Ethan's hair. "Let me talk to your daddy," she said.

"About what I said?" he asked.

She hesitated. "No. Not that."

Ethan looked at Jesse. "Okay," he said. He rose and started down the stairs, then turned and waved at Shirley. "I'll see you in Calgary," he said. Jesse watched the straight young body move swiftly down away from them. Then he sat on the bench at Shirley's feet. Her eyes were then only slightly above his.

"Ethan wants me to come back," she said.

"That's the thing you weren't going to talk about?"

He felt defensive, as if he had to quickly build protection against her.

"Yes."

"Then why talk about it?" He couldn't yield himself. Somehow it was necessary to preserve the thin calluses he'd managed to build around his feelings. He couldn't stand the pain of an open wound again. He stared out at the infield, where three cowboys drove the last of the stampede stock galloping out to the fields. When the dust settled, the arena stood as bare and empty as a country stockyard after the train has gone.

"It's about Ethan," Shirley said.

"You want him back, is that it? What about George? You never liked George as well, did you?" Though Jesse was looking away from her, he was very conscious of her knee beside his arm, and her voice scarcely the width of a hat-brim away.

"I'm not asking to take Ethan away from you," she said. "Or George either. I know what you must think of me."

What does she know? What could she know about lying alone in the darkness, waiting for the sun to rise? What could she know about a belly raw from longing—when she had great hair-covered Keno plastered there like a poultice?

"But they are still my sons. What I have done doesn't change that."

No. Nor did it change the fact that he was their father. And for that to be the case, there must have been an hour when he embraced her, an hour so buried now in folds of time and circumstance that perhaps she had forgotten. Not he.

"Please don't let Ethan be a cowboy," Shirley said.

Was that all? After everything that had happened, was that all she had on her mind? Don't let Ethan be a cowboy.

[*100*]

She hadn't changed. Sometimes, when Jesse hadn't done so well, or when he got hurt and she started to worry, she used to try to talk him out of stampeding any more. They could get a little ranch, she said. It never concerned her what they'd use for money to get the ranch. She always saw it as plain stubbornness on his part that he wouldn't do as she asked. She didn't understand the things that happen to a man when he finds he can do something better than anybody else.

"I don't see how you can even think about it," she went on. "Look what it's done to you."

What had it done to him? Broken his back. Lost him his woman. Made him into an old man with a life expectancy of forty years. On the other hand, look what it had done for Keno. It all depended on how the cards fell. Who could say that Ethan wouldn't be lucky? And the only things any father can teach his son are the things he knows.

She said, "I wanted to cry when I saw him out on that bucking steer today. What if he'd gone down under those hooves and been trampled like you were?"

But he didn't. He rode like a champ, and he collected his prize money. Ethan would become a cowboy. He had a gift. How could Jesse explain to Shirley that when you accept a gift from God, you take the whole parcel. You don't say, "Yes, Lord. I'll take the trophy. But give the pain to somebody else." You take the trophy when you are good enough to get it, and before and after and in between, you take the pain of infinite preparation, and sometimes defeat and broken bones. Does that mean you should curse God and wish he'd made you a saddle-tramp instead of a bronc-buster?

"You don't understand," Jesse said.

"That's what you used to tell me," she replied. "As if

there was some great secret to it. Keno doesn't . . ." She stopped abruptly.

Keno doesn't what? Keno doesn't pretend it's a secret? Of course he doesn't. He's not a bronc-buster; he's a businessman who happens to be able to ride bucking horses better than anybody else who is around just now. But wait till a real rider comes along—one who has the gift, who can touch his boots to those stirrups and change the whole bucking contest into an acrobatic dance, and Keno won't last five minutes. "Then talk to Keno," Jesse said. "Don't talk to me."

For a while neither of them spoke. The shadow of the grandstand stretched onto the infield now, and turned the lower portion of the white corrals to evening gray. Why was it so hard for people to talk to each other? For two years he had dreamed of a time when he might see Shirley again, and talk to her. He'd planned over and over in his mind the things he'd tell her, and sometimes when he was riding alone, he'd say them out loud. "Shirley. I can understand why you wanted to get away. I don't know why it had to be Keno, but I can see you leaving. I tell you the truth, Shirley, it's hell living without you. I know things went against us there for a while. But if you should ever feel like coming back . . ."

But what he said was, "Ethan has a gift. We think gifts from God are free, but sometimes, for them, we pay the most."

She said, "I suppose you have a gift, too?"

"I did have. Yes."

"Then it's God's fault you broke your back."

"You still don't understand, do you?"

"I don't know."

"I don't understand, either. I can't understand you

crawling in bed with that hairy bastard."

"Jesse . . ." He turned toward her, but she put her slender brown hands over her face.

Somehow he had to make her see how it was; why it was necessary for him to ruin himself, if need be; why he could not stand in Ethan's way. "The greatest thing in this world is to find out you're good at something—that you can do one thing better than any other man. It's worth anything it costs."

"Anything?" she asked.

"We don't know the cost beforehand," he said. "It's worth the risk, that's all." Was it worth losing Shirley for? "Some people are lucky."

Shirley stood up. Jesse heard footsteps on the stairs, and turned to see Keno ascending toward them.

"So there you are," Keno called as he came closer. "I've been looking all over for you."

"I'll have to go," she said. As she stepped past Jesse, her fingers rested for a moment on his shoulder. It was the only time she touched him.

Jesse turned. "Wait." Keno's boots on the stairs would have covered any last word he might say to her, but all he could think of was, Shirley, I love you. Please come back. It was too late to say that now.

Keno said, as he came up to her, "Has old Jelly-bones Jesse been moaning to you?"

Jesse couldn't speak.

"Come on, Shirl. We're late."

Jesse watched them go down the stairs, like a man and a little girl, until just before they turned the corner out of sight, the girl glanced back at him. She had the face of a woman. His woman. Then why did he let Keno have her?

CHAPTER XV

BY the time Jesse got to the Dodge, most of the cars were gone from the meadow behind the grandstand. The boys jumped out of the back seat and ran toward him.

"Is she coming?" Ethan asked.

"Who coming?"

"Mama. Is she coming back to live with us?"

"Not that I know of. Why?"

"That's what she wanted to tell you, wasn't it? That she was coming back?"

They were walking toward the car now, with Ethan holding one of Jesse's hands and George the other. J. T. sat slumped behind the wheel, even lower than usual, his hat tipped forward over his eyes. "Wait until we get home," Jesse said. "We'll talk about it then."

As they opened the car doors, J. T. pulled himself up in his seat and set his hat square on his head. "Where you been?"

"Somebody I had to see," Jesse said.

"Yeh. Ethan said you were talkin' to your ex-wife."

"She's still my wife."

As J. T. drove away, he looked across at Jesse. "Get rid of her," he said. "Get rid of her in court, so she can't come back demanding something she calls her rights. And give that feller that ran off with her a medal."

"Let's not talk about it now," Jesse said.

"She's got you in a sweat," J. T. said. "How long's she been gone? And you're still shakin' like a kid in a cathouse."

"I didn't ride so well today," Jesse said. "It was my

[*104*]

back. I've got a week till Calgary, though. I'll be in shape by then."

"You're not still in love with her, are you?"

"I said let's drop it. I won't talk about it in front of the boys."

"You don't have to worry about them," J. T. said "Any kids that have seen their ma run off with another man aren't going to get their minds bent with a little conversation."

"It's none of your business, anyway."

"If that's the way you feel about it. I was only trying to help. I've had enough experience with women; if you'd listen to me you could learn a lot."

Jesse did not reply, and they drove the rest of the way home in silence.

That night in the shack, though, the boys were full of thoughts about their mother. "She's so nice," George said.

"She said she wished we could be together again," Ethan told him.

"Well," Jesse replied. "I tried to send you, you know. You can be together with her again."

"I mean all of us," Ethan said. "All together. You and Mama and George and I."

"That's what you mean," Jesse agreed. "But what did she mean?"

"She meant the same thing."

"Did she say so? All of us—the four of us back together again?"

Ethan faltered. "Not just that way. No."

"She can come back, as far as I'm concerned," Jesse said.

"Can I tell her that?"

"No. Don't you tell her anything."

"I'd only tell her she can come back if she wants to."

"Don't tell her anything. It was her decided to go. She'll have to decide if she comes back."

George had crawled in bed, and lay very still. Ethan got in beside him, and Jesse blew out the lamp.

Jesse sat down on the side of the bed. "I know what a pigheaded kid you are," he said. Ethan's face showed dimly in the darkness. "You're like your mama. You always think you know just how things should be. And right now you're figuring out what you'll say when you see her in Calgary— tell her all about how we want her to come back. Well, that's not for you to say. She's your mother, and if she leaves you, that's too bad for you. But she's my wife, and if she leaves me, that's my business."

"Don't you love her?"

"You only ask that question because you heard J. T. ask it. And all he knows about love I could carry home in a hollowed-out BB. I've got to handle this myself. So don't say a word to her about it, or I'll have to leave you home."

"But I've got to be in the steer-riding contest."

"You don't have to do anything except stay home, if I tell you to. Now, can you talk to Shirley without making any slips?"

"Yes."

"You're sure?"

"Yes."

"You can. But will you?"

The boy hesitated. "Yes," he said at last.

George was asleep, and now his quiet breathing seemed to be the only sound in the house.

"We'll have to get a bigger bed for you and Mama," Ethan said. "It'll sure be crowded in here."

Jesse saw that Ethan understood their conversation as a sort of pact. Without realizing it, Jesse had committed himself to a plot to bring Shirley home. Perhaps it was just as well. Maybe if he admitted to himself what he was trying to do, he wouldn't blunder too badly. On the other hand, he might get nervous, and be even worse.

CHAPTER XVI

MONDAY morning the sun came up like a gong. And just as bright and brassy, Jesse and his boys jumped out of bed, put on their clothes, cooked up some porridge, ate it, whisked through the dishes, Ethan talking continually. George sang over and over again, "We're a-headin' for the Calgary Stampede," until Jesse began to wish that it had never been written. They even straightened up the house a little and swept the floor before J. T. Jones came for them.

As soon as they were in the car and on their way, J. T. asked, "How's your back?"

"It feels good this morning," Jesse said. "I've been doing some exercises for it, and that week of rest really helped. Today, I swear there's not a horse living I can't ride."

"Stay humble," J. T. told him. "I remember the last time you could ride any horse in creation." He had taken the road to the west, instead of the north. "We'll have to go the long way around. I seen a feller from Pincher Creek on Saturday—says this is the first year he's ever got stampede tickets early, and now he can't use 'em. His wife got sick— too sick to leave—so he'll have to stay home and put up hay. But if we want to pick up the tickets, we can have 'em for half price. Good seats, too. He got 'em in the mail, the middle of June."

"Well, let's pick them up," Jesse said.

They were driving on the hard surface, and getting close to Pincher Creek, when Ethan suddenly cried, "Jesse. This is where that ranch is—right along this road."

"What ranch?" Jesse asked.

"The one I told you about. The one that's for sale. The sign's just at the top of this hill."

"It's probably been sold by now."

But as they drove up the hill out of the creek, Ethan, leaning over the seat and peering through the windshield, said, "No. I can see the sign. Drive slow, Mr. Jones. Please."

J. T. slowed the car, and at the top of the hill they could see the sign, nailed to a fence post at the entrance to a grass-grown road allowance that led toward the mountains. It was a plain unfinished board, with the words printed in clumsy letters with black paint: *Ranch for Sale.* Beneath the letters was a crude arrow pointing to the west. J. T. stopped the car in front of the sign.

"Let's go look at it," Ethan said. "It's only a couple of miles up there."

"Have we got time?" Jesse asked.

"What do you want a place like that for?" J. T. said. "You'd starve to death. You get yourself some irrigated land, with pigs and sheep and a garden patch. Then at least you'll be able to eat."

The hills were green, and above them rose the mountains. "I've always wanted a cattle ranch in the foothills," Jesse said.

J. T. shrugged. "Are we going' stampedin'? Or are we shopping for cattle ranches?"

"It won't take a minute," Ethan said. "It's only a couple of miles."

J. T. put the car in gear and drove on down the road toward Pincher Creek.

"YES," Jesse said. "First, we'd better get some money."

When they got to Calgary, Victoria Park seemed quiet —more like a picnic ground than the center of a big stampede. But it wasn't yet noon. Everybody was still downtown watching the parade. After Jesse and Ethan had registered for their events, Jesse gave each of the boys fifty cents and sent them on their way, with a warning to spend their money only on rides or refreshments—they were too young for the girlie shows, and the gambling booths were crooked. Presently the crowd began to thicken, the Ferris wheel swung into motion, the merry-go-round began to play, and the lady astrologist stepped out of her tent and took a seat beneath a huge green umbrella spangled with golden rams and bulls and sea creatures. She started off by telling a gentleman in the crowd the serial number of a dollar bill he had in his pocket.

The midway interested Jesse, but he never felt comfortable on it. There had been times when he went to the freak shows and watched the man stick hatpins through his cheeks, or the crocodile girl whose eyes looked off to some far corner while she exposed her scaly body to the view of people who had paid ten cents extra to see her. He had visited Club Lido and seen other girls exhibit skin as soft as milk, but with the same expression in their eyes. It all struck him as a giant hoax. Perhaps the sword swallower was real —he must be when the neon tube he swallowed glowed red through his stomach walls—but the system that sustained him was a fraud—a panderer seeking the appearance of respectability in the shadows of the stampede. It was not until later, as he sat on the top rail of the infield corral, that he felt at home in a world he understood.

Wes Monahan, a crony from many years on the stampede circuit, came over and stood beneath him, looking up.

"You in the cow-milking, Jesse?" he asked.

"Nope."

"Want to be?"

"I'm too old for that."

"Not the way I do it," Wes said. He climbed up and sat beside Jesse. "Harry was going to milk for me, but he fell off his front porch this morning and hurt his leg. He can't run for sour apples."

"You think I can run?" Jesse asked.

"I'm lookin' for a partner," Wes went on. "If I tell you this is a sure thing, will you go in with me?"

"If you tell me it's a sure thing, I'll know you're a liar."

"I got a system. Are you in or out? I ain't tippin' my hand till you say."

The wild-cow-milking contest was a giant free-for-all—a grand melee of wild range cows, stumbling cowboys, interlocking lariats and certified confusion—supposed to be a race. A herd of cattle was turned into the arena and set upon by two-man teams of cowboys—a mounted roper and a milker on foot. While one roped and tried to hold the cow, the other had to get a few squirts of milk from her into his bottle and run with it to the judge's stand. When he was a kid Jesse competed, but after he got into the big time, it was beneath his dignity. Well, he didn't have to worry about dignity any more, and he had no objection to making a few extra dollars. "I'm in," Jesse said.

"All right," Wes said. "I'll let you in on a little secret. You see those livestock pavilions over there? Do you know they're full of dairy cows? From the time they hand out the bottles until the race starts, there's always enough lag for a man to walk that far and back."

"Are you saying what I think you're saying?"

"I have finally found out a way to take the risk out of the cow-milking contest."

[*110*]

"Are you serious?"

"Come on," Wes said. "We'll give it a dry run." He took a dollar Westclox out of his pocket. "It is now seven minutes after two."

The two of them walked around behind the chutes and corrals, across the center field of the race track, over the fence on the far side, and into the closest livestock pavilion. Here was another world. From the hurly-burly of the stampede, they entered the dignified atmosphere of prize dairy cattle. The huge barn was filled with rows of spacious stalls, each holding its cow, or bull, or cow and calf, and a few people strolled up and down the aisles between, looking at the animals.

"There you are," Wes said. "The dairy barn. You can take your pick of Jersey or Holstein, right here beside the door. Can you tell the bulls from the cows all right?"

Jesse didn't smile. He was calculating the risks involved. Wes had said that his system took the risk out of it; well, he might have something. It would sure beat trying to grab the shriveled-up tit of one of those mean old range cows, anyway.

Wes checked his watch. "A minute and a half. Now let's go back." When they were standing by the bucking chute where they had started, he said, "Four minutes. And we didn't even hurry."

Jesse looked around at the cowboys near at hand, to see who had noticed. He realized that was foolishness. With the continuous action in the arena, nobody was going to pay any attention to what he might do. Offhand, it looked like a pretty good gamble.

When the time came to start the wild-cow-milking contest, he wasn't so sure. There must be a flaw in it somewhere. If Wes had lied to him about the time lag . . . But as soon as they handed him his pint milk bottle with the number painted on the side of it—before the cows were in the arena—he knew he would at least give it a try. If it worked, it was like money from home.

As he slipped around the corner at the end of the chutes, Jesse felt as if all forty thousand people in the grandstand were watching him. But the last ride in the bareback bronc event was still going on. He needn't worry. After that, they had to drive the cattle into the arena. He had plenty of time. He found himself holding the milk bottle flat against the side of his leg, so that it was practically covered by his hand. To anybody who looked at him, he was only a cowboy walking along, though a bit too hurriedly, he suddenly realized. He deliberately slowed his pace, but tried to compensate by lengthening his stride. When he reached the cool of the barn, he was sweating. Perhaps he wasn't suited to a life of crime. He slipped into the stall closest to the door, and found a huge Holstein cow looking at him.

"Soe, bossy," Jesse said. He wished he'd chosen a Jersey. They were gentler, so he'd heard, and much smaller. If this beast took the notion, she could kick like a horse. But this was no time to be particular. He approached her from the right-hand side. "Soe, boss."

The cow shifted her hind feet and looked back at him with what must have been an expression of curiosity, but she didn't show any alarm. Jesse bent, and with his milk bottle ready, seized a starboard tit. It was about the size of a pickle jar and completely filled his hand. When he squeezed it, the milk gushed out so easily that three squirts half filled his bottle. He slipped the bottle inside his shirt, and holding it tight under his arm, he left the stall, the pavilion, and arrived back at the arena just as the milling, bellowing cows and calves were being driven in.

Wes glanced at him. He nodded. His partner smiled.

The claxon blew, and the wild-cow-milking contest had begun. The ropers galloped into the field, with their milkers running behind them. Within seconds the entire infield was a confusion of wild-eyed heifers, some running free and others lunging at the end of a lariat.

"Hurry up, Wes," Jesse shouted. "Get a rope on something." If they didn't hurry, they would lose even now. That would be funny, if the race ended with Jesse standing helpless in the arena with a bottle half full of milk.

The cattle were running in a tight circle, with their heads in close, and Wes kept waiting for one to break away and give him a good target. "Throw it!" Jesse cried. And Wes threw it. The loop settled over the surging backs, and Wes shook it to bring it down over the head of one of the cows on the edge. But at that moment a pair of horns plunged out of the melee, and one of them caught Wes's loop. In an instant his rope came tight around the base of the horn, and his prey struck out across the arena, its head tossing furiously against the pull of the rope. He'd roped a steer. Jesse ran along beside him.

"Now what'll I do?" Jesse shouted.

"Milk it!" Wes cried. "Nobody'll notice."

The steer was cavorting at the end of Wes's lariat like a wild-eyed buffalo, and Jesse was expected to milk this titless wonder. With three judges watching them, along with forty thousand witnesses, somebody was going to notice that Wes had roped a steer. If Jesse won, there might be questions asked.

"You actually got milk from a steer?"

"Yes, sir."

"Can you explain how you did it?"

"It was a bona-fide miracle."

At that moment a cow, attached to the rope of another

cowboy, came plunging across Wes's lariat, tripped, and somersaulted right in front of Jesse. There she lay for a moment, struggling on her back, with her udder turned up to the sky. Here was his miracle. Jesse reached across her flank, seized one of her tits, and while the steer and cows and other men crashed around them in the whiplash of tangled lariats, pantomimed three brisk squirts in the general direction of the bottle. Then he was off and running.

The judge's stand looked half a mile away, but Jesse ran for it on stiff, warped legs tipped into the toes of his high-heeled boots. His consolation was that probably none of the others could run any better than he. He became aware of a blur in the corner of his eye, and the sound of boots in the soft earth running up behind him. He had thought he was running as fast as he could, but suddenly his legs seemed charged with fresh energy—they galloped away with a surge that carried him full force against the chute under the judges' stand. A second later somebody else hit the boards beside him, and the puffing cowboy rasped, "You're a runnin' old fool, ain't you, Jesse?"

Almost at the same moment other competitors arrived with their little sloshes of milk, one of them loudly screaming foul. Jesse had cheated. He had stolen his milk. He hadn't milked his own cow. Jesse loudly defended himself. He had to steal his milk—his partner had lassoed a steer. The judges laughed. There weren't any steers out there. Well, see for yourselves. And they looked to see Wes, trying to flip his lariat from the horn of the big roan steer.

When Jesse saw Wes later on, he said. "Now I see why you wanted me to get my milk from the dairy barn. Do you always rope a steer in the cow-milking contest?"

"You're funny as a blister," Wes replied. "We got day money, didn't we? And we're goin' to get the big purse, too."

"You are, maybe. Not me."

"Yes, you."

"You think I'm going to get in there again with you?"

"I sure do, Jesse. That's the easiest fifty bucks you ever earned."

"I'm sorry," Jesse said. "You'll have to find yourself a new partner."

CHAPTER XVII

STAMPEDE week was off to a good start. Already Jesse had faced bad luck and come out a winner. Before Saturday night, he could expect many more sudden turns of fate, but it cheered him that he had met his first challenge. Later, during the first afternoon, he gave a winning ride in the saddle-bronc event. That'd rot old Keno's gizzard.

On Tuesday, Wes came around to continue their partnership, but Jesse firmly declined. He'd stick to his broncos.

In the saddle-bronc contest he drew a stupid old mare that plopped herself in the middle of the infield and humped her head to the east, and north, and south—as hard to ride as a fence rail. He got a reride, but the second horse was just enough better to put his back through double torture without changing the outcome. Keno took the day.

Wednesday, Jesse drew a horse called Hardtack that had a bad reputation all over the circuit. Riders liked a horse that would buck, but they didn't like them too tough. The judges scored partly on the difficulty of the horse and partly on the cowboy's performance, so it was nice to get a horse that kicked high but in a predictable pattern, so you could ride loose and still make it look good. That horse wouldn't be Hardtack. But Jesse got on his back with calm determination. Either he'd ride him and win, or fall off and lose. There wouldn't be any middle ground with Hardtack. He rode him. When it was over and the pickup man had plucked him from Hardtack's saddle, his skin was still dry and tight from the rush of fear he'd felt when the big horse erupted under him. But he'd stuck, and he'd even spurred the old monster, and at the end of the day they announced he'd won.

Thursday, Keno won. On Friday a newcomer, a kid from Rosebud, took day money in the saddle-bronc event. Jesse and Keno were both out in the cold.

On Saturday morning the doctor encased Jesse's back in wide strips of adhesive tape. It seemed to help. He needed help from somewhere. He felt as if, when he got out of bed, he had landed on the wrong foot, and now no amount of shuffling could get him in step again. He didn't even care about the contest. Why put himself through all that misery for nothing? He tried to rouse himself for another effort by remembering his hatred for Keno. His mind could remember, but his belly did not respond. The revulsion did not surge up in his throat and almost choke him as it should have done. If Keno had been old Lars himself, Jesse could scarcely have felt more neutral about him. But there it was. Keno wasn't Lars. Jesse was. It was an appropriate ending. He could go back to Gillespie's and pick up old Lars' broom, and wait for winter. It wouldn't be long coming.

When the afternoon's events began, Jesse took a seat on the top rail of the corral and tried to compose himself. His back was hurting like crazy. He didn't know if he could hang on long enough to get out of the chute. But if by some stroke of fortune, he was able to win today, his purse would be a thousand dollars. That was almost enough to buy a ranch, and four years ago at this time they had had one all picked out, up in the Porcupine Hills. Shirley had started to plan what she would do with the house, and he had decided the location for a new barn. And then came Sundown; Sundown and darkness blacker than he had ever imagined the dark could be. During the last week, though, a spark of hope had flared, and died, and flared again. Now it flickered. Another defeat might blow it out for good. Maybe he would be wise to pass this by today—let Keno take it by default, conserve his strength, and play it all for next year. He had waited so long—he could wait a little longer, couldn't he?

No, he couldn't. Every muscle in him sagged with pain and weariness. At his present rate of aging, one more year on the calendar would make him over eighty. He could never rally for another week like this had been. This was his last chance. From here on, either he would sit on his own front porch watching his cattle feed on his hillside, or he would return to San Soucie and give himself up. Was the line between heaven and hell really so thin?

Keno rode first that afternoon. He had drawn a good horse, and he gave a ride to match it—riding loose in the saddle, with one arm trailing and his spurs arcing rhythmically across the horse's shoulders. When the horn blew to end the ride, the audience came to their feet, cheering. It looked good to them, and Jesse knew it would look good to the judges, too. He might as well withdraw, and save what strength he had to wrestle with the infirmities of old age, rather than squander it in one more careening saddle. And still, as he thought these things, and felt convinced by them, he went right on buckling on his chaps and putting on his spurs. His horse today was called Polka Dot. He wondered what mad Australian monk they hired to dream up the names of these horses. Certainly the names rarely gave any indication of what a rider might expect, and Polka Dot was new to the circuit. Jesse didn't know what his bucking style was, nor could he find anybody who did.

Ethan came running up to him. "Hi," he said, smiling. Ethan had won the boys' steer-riding almost every day this week. He had good reason to smile.

"Hello, cowboy," Jesse replied.

"Mama sent you something," Ethan said, and handed him a folded slip of paper. As yet, Jesse hadn't seen Shirley since they came to Calgary.

He opened the paper and saw written there in Shirley's looping scrawl, the single word *Goldenrod*. Jesse felt a surge rush up through his body, and for a moment all his defenses were down.

"What shall I tell her?" Ethan said.

Tell her? Tell her to come back. "Did she ask you to bring an answer?"

"No. She only told me to give you that. What does it say?"

Tell her to come back, that's all. Tell her I'm going to win today, and we can buy the ranch. Tell her she doesn't have to live with Keno. There are people on this earth that love her, and she should live with them. Tell her to come back. "Tell her thanks, will you?" Jesse said.

"What does it say?" Ethan repeated.

"You wouldn't understand," Jesse said.

"Does it say she's coming home?"

"No. It's personal. You wouldn't understand."

When Ethan had gone, Jesse climbed to the top rail again, to wait for his turn in the chute. He looked at the paper in his hand. *Goldenrod*. She'd turned all his muscles to string, just at the time he needed them. *Goldenrod*. Neither of them had mentioned it for fourteen years, and now within a week or so they had both written it as a message to the other. The difference was that he had received her message while his still lay torn in little pieces like unmelted snowflakes, now scattered by the wind in J. T. Jones' pasture.

One September day the two of them had ridden into Lethbridge for a dance. They stopped on the crest of a hill and got off their horses. The prairie rolled away from them in all directions, with scarcely a tree or house or fence line in sight. And there in the field of goldenrod he'd made love to her for the first time. He could feel again the soft stalks bending under them, and smell the powdered gold dust in the air. He could see Shirley's frightened eyes, and feel her body bend to him, and in him even now there surged a sense of early manhood. That same afternoon, in the cold gray chambers of the Lethbridge City Hall, they'd been married. Through the ceremony Shirley stood like a beautiful child, clutching a spray of goldenrod beneath her throat.

For a long time Jesse had remembered that goldenrod as a reproach. How the judge must have laughed at this penniless kid who was starting married life without enough money to buy a bouquet of roses for his bride. As soon as he began to win at the stampede, he had replaced Shirley's dime-store ring with a gold one from the jewelers, but it seemed there was no way to correct the goldenrod bouquet. In time, of course, he'd forgotten about it. Now it was here again. Goldenrod.

It must have meant something to her. She didn't have to write a note to Jesse. And she could simply have said "Good luck."

"Out of chute number five!" the announcer called. "Jesse Gifford riding Polka Dot."

Polka Dot had Appaloosa blood in him. For all his pure-white front quarters, his pillow was mottled with splotches of black and muddy gray, as if he had backed up under a dripping paint brush. He was still not accustomed to the bucking chute, and as Jesse lowered himself into the saddle, Polka Dot reared and struck at the boards with his front feet. The crowd cheered. They liked a wild horse. But Jesse knew that for the kind of ride he had to have today, he needed more than action in the chute. He needed a horse that would buck. He didn't care if his back broke clean in two, and he lost his stirrup, or even if he fell off and the horse did a tap dance up his spine. If he lost today, he wanted it to be because he wasn't good enough. He wanted the whole insane business settled somehow, once and for all.

Polka Dot was down on all fours again, and Jesse thrust his boots deep into the stirrups, took a firm hold on the halter rope, pulled his hat close over his eyes, and said "Let's go." He smelled goldenrod. The gold dust of it drifted around him.

The chute clanged open. Polka Dot stood for a moment, uncertainly. Then, with the same zest he had shown earlier, he spun on his heels and leaped into the arena. Jesse felt blue sky under him, but when the horse came down hard on all four feet, he chucked back into the saddle like a rifle bolt going home. He felt as if his encasement of adhesive tape had crumbled, his pelvis smashed with the shock. But he could still swing his legs, so he knew nothing was broken. He had experienced enough pain over the past few years that a small concentration of it now wouldn't hurt him. He raised his spurs high beside Polka Dot's neck, brought them down full force into his shoulders, and raked them across his front quarters to a place in his belly behind the cinch.

Polka Dot rose in the air again. Jesse could see he was in for a high-flying, stiff-legged, jarring ride—the hardest kind for him to take right now. Every time Polka Dot landed, it felt as though his spine was telescoping, until soon his head would sit directly on the saddle. But if his body was only six inches long, they could get by with a much smaller coffin. And if that coffin lid was waiting to close over him, he might as well ride while he could. He clinched his teeth and swung his legs back and forth, spurring Polka Dot, while the horse lunged more and more desperately, squealing with fury. For a few moments the forty thousand people were gone. There were only the two of them—Polka Dot and Jesse, struggling alone in a cloud of dust from the goldenrod. When the horn blew to mark the end of the ride, it seemed also to call Jesse back from another world—a place of dedication and pain. And though he became aware of the pickup man galloping close beside him, he had not strength to reach out for help. Rather, his whole body collapsed. He rolled from the saddle and fell face-first in the dust, and the earth beneath him shook again and again, each time more faintly as Polka Dot's thumping hooves retreated.

CHAPTER XVIII

AS soon as the afternoon events were over, J. T. was ready to go home, but Jesse put him off. Why not wait till evening and see the chuck-wagon races? J. T. murmured that his farm had been standing empty for a week, and heaven only knew what could have happened to it by now; but he stayed. After the chuck-wagon races, there was a stage show—musicians and dancers and acrobats and comedians performing on the open-air stage in front of the grandstand. The long twilight ended during the first few acts, and darkness gathered around the stage, heightening the effect of light and swirling color. Ethan and George were enthralled by the dancing bear, and J. T. even forgot his impatience during the high-wire act.

As the orchestra screamed out the finale, and the dancing girls kicked what appeared to be their last, J. T. rose to go, but Jesse reminded him that the awards ceremony was next, and they might as well wait for that. J. T. grumpily suggested that this was all Jesse had been waiting for, anyway, which may have been at least partly true. They agreed to meet back at the car, and Jesse left to join the rest of the cowboys gathering on the stage. Onto the floor just vacated by men wearing tuxedos and lithe girls in sequined costumes, the cowboys nudged each other, hobbling like bowlegged penguins, ten-gallon hats sitting over their eyes or held in fumbling hands in front of their shirts. This was not their element. All the power and grace they had displayed in the arena seemed to have been left in the barn with their horses.

One by one they were called out of the wide semicircle they had formed across the stage, to come front and center to receive their trophies. Wes accepted the cup for the wild-cow-milking contest with humility and gratitude, just as though he'd been through proper hell to win it. For Jesse, the hell he had felt during his ride on Polka Dot had paid off. He had beaten Keno. Jesse was the winner that day, and with his presentation, the president of the Stampede Board gave a little sermon on courage and the thrill of watching a real comeback, until Jesse became so embarrassed he almost wished he'd gone home with J. T. Jones five hours ago. Still, the applause that welled out of the dark stands and flowed down over him was good to hear. He accepted the silver-mounted saddle and the check, and returned to stand with the other cowboys, the trophy on his shoulder. One thousand dollars. One thousand dollars in one lump. That brought his winnings for the week to fourteen hundred; for the summer, to seventeen or eighteen hundred dollars. For a moment he felt tall again—so tall he could see right over the grandstand, over the lights of the Ferris wheel, over the miles of dark hills to a valley still green in the sunlight—a place where darkness never came. He'd buy that valley now, and bask in its sun for the rest of his life.

The awards had scarcely been completed when the sky flared white and crackled with the opening burst of fireworks. Jesse had wanted to be with George for the fireworks display—it would be the first he'd ever seen—but the crowd was filing down from the grandstand, jamming the area around the stage shoulder to shoulder with people, their upturned faces repeatedly illuminated by the colored flashes. He became aware that someone was shouting at him. It was Wes. "At the Wales!" Jesse heard him say. "Room 403. Stop by for a drink."

"Sure!" Jesse called back. "Sure. Thanks." Wes pushed on through the crowd, calling to some of the other cowboys. A drink sounded like a good idea. That was one delay that J. T. should accept with pleasure.

When the fireworks had ended, the crowd thinned quickly, like water running into cracks in the ground, and Jesse crossed the parking lot through a whirling galaxy of auto lights to find J. T. and the boys waiting for him beside the car. George was so tired, he immediately crawled onto the back seat and went to sleep.

"Wes Monahan would like us to stop by his room for a drink," Jesse said.

"I don't know any Wes Monahan," J. T. replied, "but

I can tell right off he's my kind of man. I been waiting all night to hear a good excuse for hanging around this town."

"The Wales Hotel," Jesse said. They were in the car and moving now, and as Jesse glanced back he saw on his older son's face, white in the glare, signal weariness and disappointment at the plan. "We'll only be a minute," Jesse assured him. "You won't have to wait long."

Ethan shrugged. "It's all right," he said. He slumped back across his brother's legs and turned his face to the side window, though from that angle he could have seen nothing but the fringes of light arcing beneath the sky.

In the lobby of the Wales Hotel was a sign which said *No visitors after 11 p.m.* On another wall, a large pendulum clock told them it was forty-five minutes to midnight. But there were people milling in the lobby, running up and down the stairs, ringing for the elevator, arguing with the clerk at the desk. If there were guests who wanted to sleep, Jesse trusted that they had been given rooms on the top floor. When he and J. T. got to room 403, the door was open, spilling some of its occupants into the hall—mostly cowboys and their wives, people Jesse knew or had known in days gone by. Inside the room there were people sitting on the bed, the chairs, the desk, the window sill, and standing in overlapping clusters, while Wes dispensed drinks from the dresser top.

With so many voices crowding the room, and such frequent and unrestrained bursts of laughter, it seemed impossible to understand what anybody was saying. But when he saw Jesse, Wes made himself heard. "Well!" he cried. "Here's the champ! Quiet, please. Quiet, everybody!" There was a slight subsidence of uproar, which caused those who hadn't heard Wes to glance over their shoulders. Within a moment or two the room had become completely quiet.

"You know this ain't intended to be a formal occasion,"
Wes said. "Just a gatherin' of friends. But I reckon a host
has privileges, and tonight it's my privilege to propose a
toast to an old friend of mine—a fella with more guts than
a slaughterhouse—you may be able to bust his back, but
you'll never dint his spirit—the man with the carborundum
grit, and still the best damn bronc rider I ever did see—
Jesse Gifford!"

The assembly drank; there was a short, sporadic cheer,
a couple of cries for a speech, and a moment of confused
uncertainty. Then Wes shouted, "Come on, Jesse. We just
wanted to be sure everybody had one drink before you
started. I got one for you here that would raise hair on a
brass saddle horn." Jesse passed through the crowd toward
Wes, and the moment passed, the halted conversation began to move again. Jesse felt more comfortable.

He left Wes talking to J. T., and began to move through
the room, greeting old friends from the rodeo circuit. It felt
good to be a kind of celebrity among these people he re-
spected. As he stood with lowered head, listening and talking, he raised his eyes and saw Shirley only a few steps away,
facing him. She still looked so young, as though the years
that had rolled over him had left her untouched. She came
toward him with her hand extended, her lips saying the
word "Congratulations." In the hubbub the sound was lost.

"Thanks," he said. The warm pressure of her hand
continued, as if to bridge the gap left by the formality of
their words. She said something more. "What?" he asked,
bending his head closer to her.

In the same quiet voice she said, "You looked good out
there today."

"Do you think so?"

"I never saw you give a better ride."

"Well, thanks," he said. "That's good to hear." The

pressure of her hand and her sudden closeness had aroused him, and he wanted to say something intensely personal to her, but no words would come. At last he said, "I got your note."

"You understood it? You hadn't forgotten?"

"It was powerful."

"I didn't know what to put. I mean, you know . . ." In the midst of the din, they had achieved a sudden intimacy, like two eggs in a cocoon surrounded by flossy layers of sound which sealed them against the world beyond. Shirley went on speaking. "I know I'm supposed to be wicked, but I don't feel wicked. I only feel mixed up, and sometimes lonely. But I wonder what you think of me, and I never know what to say to you any more. It all seems to come out twisted. Even 'Goldenrod.' "

"I got it straight. It made the difference."

"Really?"

"I had about decided not to ride at all today."

"Then it was all right?"

"It was the best medicine I've had in years." Directly beneath his lowered eyes, in the V made by the collar of her blouse, he could see the firm, round parting of her breasts. "Come home with us," he said.

"Not yet. I can't come yet."

"But soon?"

"I don't know."

"We need you. Not only me. The boys need you, too."

"I know. I feel so miserable."

"I'm going to buy a ranch," Jesse said.

"You are?"

"Got it all picked out. Ethan found it, really." Jesse laughed. "He ran away from home one night, and came back all excited about this ranch he'd found."

"Ran away?" she cried. "Why did he run away?"

"It wasn't anything," he said quickly, knowing he'd blundered. "He didn't actually run away—just went for a ride to cool off. He gets mad at me sometimes, too, you know."

"The crazy little kid." She looked up, then leaned toward him, even closer than before. "Why would he want to run away?"

"It's in the foothills," he went on. "Right on the main road. Or close to it, anyway. With a creek, a log house."

"It's all my fault, isn't it? I've ruined it for all of us— you and Ethan and George . . . And me, too. I've ruined it for me as much as anyone."

"It's all right. You can come home with us tonight."

"If only I could. I've made such terrible mistakes, it seems I'm afraid to do anything any more."

"I think about you every night. I never go to sleep without thinking about you."

"Oh, Jesse . . ." Her voice stopped abruptly, and Jesse looked up to find Keno standing beside them.

"Well, I hope I'm not interrupting anything," Keno said, so loudly that his voice seemed to ride above all the other sounds in the room, until they faded to a murmur, and then stopped completely.

A moment before, Jesse had been alone with Shirley, but now the whole world watched them. Keno seemed uncomfortably aware that he was causing a scene. At first he looked as though he might continue to play it out, but he hesitated, and a shadow, as of doubt, passed across his face. When he spoke again, his voice was almost a whisper. "It's time to go home," he said. His big hand closed on Shirley's arm and turned her toward the door. Jesse stood flat-footed and watched them leave the room.

The party seemed to shudder and die. The smoke hung like a shroud partway down from the ceiling, and people turned pale faces toward each other as if in search of a spark that could give life to the room again. None was found. Though efforts were made, the laughter that accompanied them came across more as a mourner's wail, and only deepened the silence that followed it. Jesse found J. T. Jones. "Ready to go?" he asked quietly. J. T.'s haste appeared to have run itself out; he didn't care if he stayed or went. Wes was full of apologies—he shouldn't have invited Keno, but he just didn't think . . . It was all right, Jesse told him. In fact, it was the best thing that had happened to him all day. He and J. T. walked down the hall and were soon on the street outside.

There was an old man on the sidewalk by the door, dressed in a cap and greatcoat, as though it were a winter night. *"Albertan,"* he said. "Morning *Albertan.*" Jesse bought a copy and opened it under the light from the hotel window. There on the front was a picture of Jesse Gifford receiving his trophy saddle. "Cowboy Cops Crown in Rangeland Classic." He folded the paper again, put it under his arm, and followed J. T. toward the Dodge.

On the long drive home, Jesse tried to stretch out across his half of the front seat, but no matter which way he turned he could not relieve the pressure on his pelvic bone. It almost felt as if it had been broken again. But even while he writhed, he whistled to himself. In his pocket was a check for a thousand dollars, and in the trunk of the car, wrapped in burlap, was a silver-mounted saddle engraved to Jesse Gifford, Saddle Bronc Champion. Tomorrow he would tack the front page of the *Albertan* to the wall above his head. Then he would lie there for a thousand years and try to imagine how Keno felt when he opened the paper that morning. Wouldn't it stick in his craw to have his picture shoved off the front page by a worn-out old cripple like Jesse? Take that, Keno you bastard. Do you think a woman with Shirley's class wants to hang around with a has-been? And when you climb in bed tonight with your prick all shriveled up like a peanut, what do you think will happen? First shoved off the front page; then shoved out of bed. Keno, you poor old bastard.

As the car droned on through the darkness, though, Jesse began to feel like a disembodied spirit, lost in a world made wholly of darkness and pain. It became harder for him to remember the check in his pocket, or the saddle in the trunk, or his picture on the front page of the newspaper. His hour of triumph had come, and now it was gone, and he had no hope for another. A saddle and a thousand dollars and his picture in the paper would have to last him for the rest of his life. And perhaps they would. It depended on what he could do with them.

The car finally stopped, and Jesse rose up to see the headlights shining on his stable at the end of the lane. They were home. J. T. wakened the boys, and they walked unsteadily into the house. Jesse would have preferred to crawl, but it hardly seemed a suitable posture for the champ, so he hobbled in as quickly as he could and flung himself on the bed. He heard J. T. clump his trophy saddle down in the kitchen, and then after a moment or two the headlights shone into his room as the car turned around, and the sound of it faded off into the night.

The boys were asleep again, lying in bed with their clothes on. Jesse roused himself enough to take off their shoes; then he pulled the covers over their shoulders,

and again lay back on his own bed. That was all he needed
—to really stretch out. Already the pain in his back was
beginning to ease.

He was the Champ. There was nobody else as good at
his business on this globe.

CHAPTER XIX

FOR the next few days, while Jesse lay around nursing his
back, it seemed the only topic of conversation was "the
ranch." Even J. T. was brought into the discussions. He
tried to talk Jesse into buying irrigated land, where, as he
put it, a man could make a living. But Jesse didn't want to
spend his springtime sloshing through an irrigated field in
gum boots, or his summer hoeing in a potato patch, or
milking a half-dozen cows night and morning just for the
sake of a creamery check once a week—might as well clean
out San Soucie's horse barn for the rest of his life as tie
himself down to a slave camp like that. He pictured hills
covered with buffalo grass and cattle, and if it meant doing
day work to bring in a little money, he was willing.

Ethan campaigned for the ranch at Twin Butte. And
one morning J. T. came over to ask Jesse if he'd like a ride
over to Pincher Creek. "I got to take an extree into the
blacksmith's."

"You mean, and look at the ranch?"

"That's what I was thinking of."

"Let's go, Jesse," Ethan exclaimed.

"Oh, I don't think you kids would want to go," J. T.
said. "What would you do in town all afternoon?"

"Wait, I guess," Ethan replied. "We want to go."

It was clear that J. T.'s invitation had not been meant to include the boys, but Jesse couldn't go looking for a ranch without Ethan. If J. T. made an issue of it, they'd all have to stay home. "They wouldn't be any trouble," Jesse said.

"I don't care what you do," J. T. replied. "Bring your horses and dogs too, if you want. I'll pick you up about noon." He walked out of the house and drove away.

Shortly after lunch the four of them were headed west toward the mountains. They traveled for several miles, crossed the Waterton River, drove up a long hill past the Yarrow Church, from which, it was said, you could see for fifty miles in any direction. To the south and west, the view was cut short by the mountains, but the blue hump of the Porcupine Hills was visible far to the north, and east of them the prairie faded across an immense distance, until at the horizon only a shadow of the Milk River Ridge could be seen.

A few miles after they turned north on the Waterton–Pincher road, they came to the sign nailed to a fence post. "It's still there," Ethan cried.

"I'm running late," J. T. said. "I tell you what. I'll let you off here, and pick you up on my way home." No doubt J. T. had planned a day spent wandering from pool hall to beer parlor to cathouse. The two boys would put a crimp in his style, so he was ditching Jesse too. Jesse got out of the car, the boys behind him, and J. T. drove swiftly on his way. He said nothing about what time he would be back for them.

When the sound of the Dodge had faded over the hill, the quiet came down like a curtain—a quiet deepened by the gradual awareness of insect noises and an awesome rushing sound, neither wind nor water, that seemed to flow out of the mountains. Near at hand a grove of aspens rustled like the sound of a man turning over in a straw bed, and the sudden breeze that shook them cooled Jesse's face as it passed.

"Come on," Ethan said. He had started up the road, but called back to Jesse and George. Jesse looked down at his younger son, whose face was tipped toward the mountains as if he were caught in a spell.

"Shall we go?" Jesse said. George put his hand out to his father, and hand in hand they followed Ethan deeper into the hills. "How far is it?" Jesse asked.

"A couple of miles, maybe," Ethan said. "I didn't really notice."

The road allowance ended, with a gate across it, and from there the two dirt tracks in the grass wound over the hills. Each time they topped a rise, Jesse expected to find the ranch buildings, but all they could see was the track leading through another swail and over another crest. Finally, though, the road dipped sharply toward a creek, and then flattened on a bench which held a squat log cabin and a few outbuildings. Further back among the trees, Jesse could see the roof of a hay barn. "There she is," Ethan said. The mountains seemed to bend above them.

"Can we buy it, Jesse?" Ethan asked.

They walked down the hill. "How do I know? They might have a thousand acres. I don't know."

"I hope we can," Ethan said. "It's got trees and a creek. I'll bet you could catch fish in that creek."

"I wouldn't be surprised," Jesse agreed.

"I'll catch fish every day," Ethan said. "That'll save us quite a bit."

They were close to the bottom of the hill now. George took Jesse's hand again. "What do you think, George?" Jesse said.

[*132*]

"It's so far away," the little boy said.

"Far away?" Ethan asked. "Far away from where?"

"Anywhere," George said. "It's just far away."

As they drew near the cabin, its door opened and a woman stepped out. Three girls slipped around her and lined up against the log wall, staring at Jesse and the boys. Jesse kept walking until he was perhaps twenty feet away. Then he stopped and took off his hat. Crinkles of white ran into the woman's brown face from around her eyes, appearing and disappearing as she alternately sobered and grimaced in the glare of the sun. Her eyes were gray, lost in the weathered pattern of her face.

"Howdy, ma'am," Jesse said.

The woman nodded.

"You got a ranch for sale?"

She nodded again.

"We came to see it."

"Have a look," she said.

Jesse turned his head slowly, first to the right and then to the left viewing the creek and the barn, the log house with its broad flat eaves, and over all the mountains. "How much land?" he asked.

"They's a half-section. Hay and pasture land." When she talked, she paused after every few words, pursed her lips, and then continued.

"We'll look around," Jesse said.

She pressed her thin lips together twice before she spoke. "They's a harse in the barn if you want to ride. They's only one there, though. Yer can't all ride."

"Is the place fenced?" Jesse asked.

"Yer can tell where it is. Hit's the south half. They's a fence hall the way round it, and a cross-fence down the middle. Yer standin' in the southwest quarter. Hall the cattle yer see belong—'bout sevnny-five head, or so. Half a dozen harses."

"We'll see you in a while," Jesse said. "After we have a look."

The woman nodded and pressed her lips. She and the girls remained in front of the cabin, watching them go.

They got the horse out of the barn. Jesse and George rode, while Ethan ran beside them, along the creek and over the hills. "It's perfect," Ethan said after a while. "Isn't it, Jesse?" He was puffing slightly.

The buildings were half falling down. The fences needed repair. The hay should have been cut two weeks ago. "Pretty near," Jesse replied. "It's almost perfect." For a while he even forgot about his back.

Later they returned the horse to the stable and strolled around the barnyard. In the grass on a high creek bank, a few pieces of machinery stood in various stages of decay, so that it was hard to tell what was still serviceable. The bull wheel of a rusty old binder was half buried in the earth; it could not have been moved for years. But on the hay rake Jesse could see a couple of places where remnants of red paint still remained. The mower stood by itself at one side, its cutter bar raised, its grass-board trailing like a banner. But for all its proud silhouette, the mower was old. The contours of its iron body gleamed from the stroke of countless brittle stalks of hay. Its tongue had been broken, and spliced with boards wired like splints on either side. Whoever parked the machine here at the end of last summer's haying season had not even removed the knife, but left it standing in the elements all winter. Now it looked as if it might be fused to the cutter bar with rust.

Further along they passed under some trees and came to the hay barn, a long, narrow roof set on a log superstructure, like scaffolding. It had been built into a hillside, so that one end of the roof butted directly against the steeply sloping grass, and the other soared thirty feet above the ground. On the floor of the barn now, far beneath the roof, the remains of last year's hay crop lay in sunken heaps, bleached and musty.

"Well. What do you think?" Jesse asked.

"Perfect," Ethan said. "Don't you think so?"

"It's too far away," George said.

"Let's go see what she wants for it," Jesse said.

The door of the cabin opened as they approached, and the woman invited them in. The interior was cramped and dark. Though it was larger than their place at J. T. Jones', it seemed smaller because of all the furniture, boxes, antlers, trunks, and papers that had accumulated in it. The log walls were almost black, and the mortar in the cracks was gray with age and the smoke from the kitchen stove.

"Set down," the woman said. She pursed her lips and tucked a loose strand of hair into the bun at the back of her head.

Jesse and Ethan each sat on one of the straight-backed chairs, and George sidled between his father's legs. "Your husband home?" Jesse asked. The woman sat down across the table from him. Her girls stood lined against the wall, the taller one cutting down the light that came through the window.

"My husband's daid," the woman replied. "He died in the winter. I'se glad, Lord forgive me. He died, and I'm goin' to heaven—back home to Manitoba." She sighed. "They was a blizzard on. We couldn't get to town. The ground was froze. We tried all day to dig it. It was too hard. And the wind drifted the snow faster than we could dig. It was gettin' dark. I didn't know what to do."

She looked at Jesse, her lips working. Her eyes kept sliding off him. "I'se scared of that man. I'se scared of him alive, and I'se scareder of him daid. I could sleep better with the devil himself in the cabin with me." She hesitated. "We stuffed him through a hole in the ice. I chopped a hole, and the water was black. We stuffed him in, and I ain't been down the creek all summer. I jest been settin' here prayin'. Ain't planted no garden. Ain't cut no hay. Jest milk the cow and pray is all I done. And finally you come. You buy this ranch, you're an angel, mister. The hand of the Lord done it." She pressed her lips and pushed at her hair.

"How much are you asking?" Jesse said.

"Two thousand, five hundred dollars." Then she added, "Cash."

"I haven't got that much money," Jesse said.

"You got any money?"

"Sure he's got money," Ethan said. "He's Jesse Gifford, the saddle-bronc champion."

The woman looked at him, her mouth working. "That right?"

"Yes. I'm Jesse Gifford."

"But that other thing?"

"Yes. I'm that, too."

"How much money you got?"

"Fifteen hundred dollars." Counting what Ethan had won, he had a little more than that, but he didn't want to start ranching flat broke.

"Cash?"

"Yes."

"Thank the Lord. I'll take it."

Jesse didn't know what to say.

The woman opened the drawer of the kitchen table and took out a large, crisp piece of paper. Carefully, as if it were a centuries-old parchment, she unfolded it. "I got this out of the trunk the other day," she said. "Case somebody come along. It's the Duplicate Certificate of Title." She handed it to Jesse. "Everythin' free and clear."

The title granted to Mable Gunderson an estate in fee simple, and described the section, township, and range west of the fifth meridian, containing three hundred and twenty acres more or less. It was dated May 27, 1919.

"Are you talking about a going concern?" Jesse asked.

"Lock, stock, and barrel. We won't take nothin' with us but the clothes on our backs."

It was a bargain—a bailing-wire bargain. They might take a while to get it in shape, but Jesse had lots of time. "How come it's in your name?" he said.

"I bought it, with my own money that my pa left me. Gunder never had nothin'. He come home from the war all dressed up in his uniform, full of big talk and plans fer his cattle empire, as he called it. I'se just a silly girl in them days, and I believed him. My brothers tried to tell me . . ." She shook her head. "He wanted it in his name, but I never done that, thank the Lord." She bowed her head for a moment as if to verify the thanks. "They's fellers around here wantin' the ranch all right, but they ain't got a dime to their backs. They just want to marry me and keep me here like Gunder done, workin' till I drop. But I ain't goin' to stay. Seventeen years I been here in the black shadow of them mountains. And Gunder standin' over me. And never draw breath and call it mine. No more. I'se a pretty girl when I'se eighteen years old."

Jesse looked at Ethan. "It'll be a big job," he said.

The boy's eyes were bright with excitement, but in the presence of female strangers he must have felt the need for dignity. "We can do it," he replied.

The woman had even gotten a printed bill of sale from the store. Jesse wondered if she was really as simple as she pretended. He filled out the form according to the information on the title and what she told him about livestock, goods, and chattels. When he was finished, she didn't even read it—just took the pen and laboriously wrote her name in the blank provided: *Mable Gunderson.*

"We need a witness," Jesse said.

"We'll stop at the lawyer's office when you take me to Pincher. We got to catch the train at six-thirty. Can you drive us in the democrat?"

"Today?" Jesse asked.

"Right now," the woman said. "We been packed for months. We're ready to go." The woman rose and dragged a trunk out of the corner. "Get your things," she said to the girls. They disappeared into one of the bedrooms. "They's a democrat behint the barn," she said to Jesse. "Time you get it hitched, we'll be ready."

"Don't you want your money?"

She paused in her hurried preparations, and looked at him. "I forgot," she said. She sat down again.

Jesse reached inside his shirt and pulled the money belt from around his body. One by one he emptied the pockets in it and counted the bills onto the table in front of her. "Fifteen hundred dollars," he said at last.

The woman placed her hand over the untidy stack of bills as if a sudden breeze might blow them away. "The Lord's hand is in it," she said and tucked the money in the pocket of her dress.

"Did they find your husband?" Jesse asked.

"No. I ain't told nobody. And I ain't been down the creek myself."

"I think you'd better let the Mounties know."

GOLDENROD

"I'll tell 'em when I get to town," she said.

They brought around the rubber-tired democrat, loaded the trunk and boxes into it, and Ethan prepared to drive the women to Pincher Station, while Jesse and George stayed behind in case J. T. should call for them. As soon as they were all seated, either on boxes or on the trunk, Ethan flipped the lines and clicked his tongue, and the democrat rolled silently away, moving on its rubber tires with a hint of luxury, for all its lack of springs or padded seat. "Be sure you stop at the lawyer's," Jesse called after Ethan. "Leave the papers with him and ask him to register the title."

The woman looked back over her shoulder, her face turned down, but her eyes raised as if the mountain were about to fall and she was escaping just in time. "Thank the Lord," she said. "I can't believe that in a couple of days I'll be home in Manitoba."

CHAPTER XX

JESSE watched the democrat pull over the hill and out of sight. He felt stunned. For the first time in his life the ground beneath his boots belonged to him, and somehow the whole earth had changed. He was no longer a gladiator struggling in the dust of the arena for other people's amusement; he was a partner in God's creation. This three-hundred-and-twenty-acre corner of the great earth now waited for him.

"Come on," he said to George. "Let's see if we can get that old mower ready to go." Hand in hand, they walked across the barnyard. Hay to cut, fence to fix, calves to brand —he'd have to register his brand now—harness to mend,

[139]

body down the creek. He hoped they remembered to tell the Mounties about the dead man. Jesse surely didn't want to be the first to come across him.

The grass had grown up so thick beneath the mower that when he let down the cutter bar and released the Pitman, and tried to pull out the knife, the rusty sections became plugged and wouldn't move. Only by pushing the knife forcibly back and forth several times, was he finally able to mangle the grass enough that he could pull the knife out. As he stood it on end and looked at it, he wondered whether he should have saved himself the trouble. Along its four-foot length, at least three sections were broken. If there were some new sections somewhere, of course, it could quickly be fixed, but if there had been some available, why would the gentleman down the creek have tried to mow with this snaggle-toothed knife instead of fixing it? The best he could hope for was to find a whetstone somewhere.

He started toward the old log shop. It was covered with rings and wheels and bits of chain and broken haywire that hung from its sides like scales. Gunderson had apparently been the sort who never throws anything away. Just as Jesse was about to step inside the door to look for a hand sharpener, his eye caught sight of one of a different kind, and he stopped. Sitting in the sun beside the shop was a wheel grinder. He sat down on the narrow board saddle and pressed the treadle with his foot. The grinder, like a giant stone dollar suspended on edge between his knees, did a slow quarter-turn around its axle.

George put his hands over his ears. "Ooh," he said. "It squeaks."

"It squeaks," Jesse agreed, "but it turns." He lifted the mower knife into a horizontal position, holding it as he might a balancing pole if he were riding a bicycle over

Niagara Falls. Then he pressed the treadle down, let it up, pressed it down . . . The wheel of the grinder began to turn, screeching on two melancholy notes as if it cried out, first in pain, and then relief, each time he worked the treadle. He brought the knife carefully down, so that the whirling stone struck against the edge of one rusty section. There was a sharp, grating noise, and a spray of sparks shot out from the point of contact.

"Wow!" George cried.

Jesse sighed. He had found one thing on the ranch that worked. Inside the shop was a grimy oilcan, and with it he was able to tone down, though not end, the squeaks of the grinder. Then he sat down and went to work. The grinder turned more easily since it had been oiled, and now, as the sound of stone on metal rose again, the sparks flew out like the curved tail of a comet, and a few of them followed the stone all the way around, so it appeared to be circled with a slender rim of fire.

Jesse settled himself comfortably to sharpen the sections and grind a cutting edge on the broken ones. He still felt stunned. It was difficult to believe that two hours ago he had been a bum; now he was a rancher, a landowner, a taxpayer, a solid citizen with a half section of land and a wheel grinder.

He had promised Shirley a ranch. He would have promised her anything, of course, but he had been sincere about the ranch. There had been no question in his mind that he would have it, and soon. It had taken longer than he expected—too long, as it turned out. Now he had the ranch, but it seemed the reason for it was gone. Still, it was salvation for Jesse, pure and simple—salvation from San Soucie's particular brand of hell. Glory and salvation all at once.

Why couldn't she have waited another year or two?

Maybe the ranch wouldn't have made the difference, but in his mind it did. It hadn't been Keno himself, but Keno's ranch and Keno's championship. Before Sundown, Jesse had been next in line for all those things. If he'd got them then, he'd still have Shirley. Now what was he to do with them?

She'd never asked for any promises. He was a green cowhand and she was the boss's niece, come from Wyoming to spend the summer. She helped her aunt fix meals for the cowboys and take care of the house. After supper one night he'd begged off from a horseshoe game and strolled down the lane where he knew she sometimes walked in the evening. He'd missed quite a few horseshoe games after that. "Jesse would rather pitch woo than horseshoes." "You made any ringers yet, Jesse?" "You ain't careful, Jesse, the next ring you get'll be on her finger, and in your nose." Jesse didn't mind. Rather, it pleased him to be joshed about Shirley. It was a public acknowledgment that she was his girl, and as long as that was so, he didn't care about anything else.

And one summer night under a big tree that grew down the slope from the ranchhouse, he'd lain with his head in her lap and talked about the ranch they'd have: not too big, a couple of sections maybe, but good land, with lots of white-faced cattle. There'd be a big red barn by the river, with a weathervane like an iron horse swinging from the peak of it. The house would be on higher ground, but still where they could see the water from the living room. The upstairs windows would look over the roof of the veranda that went all the way around the front of the house. In the summer the organdy curtains would blow back and forth in the open windows. From the high branch of a tree in front of the house, he'd make a swing with a length of old hay rope, where Shirley, and later on her babies, could fly thirty feet above the ground.

"It sounds beautiful," Shirley said. "But I don't care whether the barn's red, or the house has a porch, or even if I can only swing twenty feet high. If I can live there with you, that's all I want."

Well, there was only a half section of land. The cattle that were to have been white-faced were either brockel-faced or spotted. The barn wasn't red. It was weathered old logs with a straw roof that needed replacing. There wasn't even a tree big enough to swing a twenty-foot rope from. But it was his. It was where he lived, and if Shirley knew about it, wouldn't she live here too?

Hah! What difference would a down-at-the-heels patch of foothills make to her? It wasn't digging a garden that Shirley wanted now. One day perhaps, but no longer. It wasn't patching overalls the third time around. It wasn't sweeping a plank floor with a widow lady's worn-out broom. Jesse must be insane to think that a haywire outfit like this could make her want to come back. He had to give that widow lady credit. She had flummoxed him in five minutes, and now here he was, stuck with fifty ton of hay waiting to be cut, and a cow to be milked night and morning—nothing to show for his prize money but a three-hundred-and-twenty-acre slave camp. He had set a trap for Shirley, and all he caught was himself.

He turned the mower knife over. The cutting edges of the sections gleamed in a silver zigzag against the ugly brown rust, the pattern broken occasionally by a section with the point broken off. He took the oilcan along with him back to the mower. He oiled the knife, the cutter bar, the Pitman, the gearbox, the wheels. Now, as he slid the knife into place, it smoothly clipped the grass which stood between the guards. "Yes sir, George," he said. "I think as soon as Ethan gets back with the team, we're ready to cut hay."

"Now Mama will come home, won't she, Jesse?"

"Why? Who told you that?"

"Ethan. He said if we had a ranch, Mama would come home."

"Well, it's a lie. Mama isn't coming home."

It was almost dark when Ethan drove into the yard, his team walking with heads down and tails hanging straight. He pulled the horses to a stop in front of the barn. Then he and Jesse unhooked the tugs, dropped the tongue of the democrat, and undid the neck yoke. "Did you go to the lawyer's?" Jesse asked.

"Yup. He said he'd take care of everything for us."

"And she caught her train all right?"

"She sure did. You'd have thought somebody was after her."

"Maybe she pulled a fast one," Jesse said. "But she couldn't fake the title. As long as she is Mable Gunderson, and as long as they didn't mortgage the place after this title was made, I can't see how she could have fleeced us."

"She sure seemed to keep looking over her shoulder."

They led the team of horses into the barn, and Jesse and Ethan each unharnessed one of them.

"Mama's coming home now, isn't she?" George asked again.

"I think she is," Ethan said.

"What do you tell him stuff like that for?" Jesse said. "You only make him unhappy."

"But I think she is," Ethan replied.

"Well, she's not. So forget it."

"How do you know?"

"I know."

"She didn't ask you when she went," Ethan said. "Does she have to let you know when she's coming back?"

The team, turned loose now, walked slowly out of the stable. The sun was down. In the strange, unreal light of evening, the heavy beasts lowered themselves to the ground, and groaning wearily, rolled in the dust of the barnyard.

Jesse heard a car horn sounding impatiently at the top of the hill—it was probably J. T. come to pick them up. As he started walking up the road to meet J. T., Jesse called back over his shoulder, "You boys better go see where they put the lamp or we'll be eating our supper in the dark."

He returned in a few minutes to find George squatting down in front of the cabin, as if he were still unsure of where he belonged in this new place. "Was that J. T.?" he asked.

"It was him all right. He thought I was crazy to buy a place like this, and maybe he's right. Anyhow, he went off in a huff. I told him we'd fetch our things in a week or two, but for now, the first thing we have to do is mow some hay." Jesse thought about the outline of the hay barn, high and black against the sky. "Think we can fill that old barn with hay before the snow flies?"

"Sure we can," Ethan said.

CHAPTER XXI

JESSE had never known a morning like the one that followed. The sunlight that struck the slopes of the hills looked as heavy as if it had been taken from a palette; as if, should you touch it with your fingers, they'd come away yellow. He dressed quietly, and left the boys still sleeping while he went to milk the cow and harness the team. As he crossed the yard, milk bucket on his arm, he felt a peace sink down in him that he had never known before. All his life he had been either scrambling to reach the top or scratching to keep alive. Now all at once he was beyond those, living in a safe new world, where after less than twenty-four hours he felt at home.

While he milked, he thought of the things he must do to make this world secure. The first thing was to fill that barn with hay. It looked as though it would hold fifty ton; that would be a big job for two boys and a man with a half-broken back, but if they were to be sure of getting their cattle through the winter, it had to be done. And they'd need their things from J. T. Jones; they couldn't wear the same pair of socks forever.

It seemed that there was something else bothering him. When he went to the pasture to catch the horses he remembered what it was. He looked in a quiet pool of the creek, and he remembered the man who had been buried there. Where was that man now? Hooked on a branch somewhere, his body bloated and his skin turned blue? There seemed to be a blemish in the air—a hint of decay he hadn't noticed before.

The haying went well. The mower worked. They found the remnants of a set of harness, and by stringing together every scrap of leather on the place with copper rivets they found in the shop, they outfitted another team of horses. While Jesse mowed, Ethan raked the hay into windrows to dry, and a day or two later, cocked it. Within a few days they were ready to start stacking. Jesse had not forgotten the other things on his list of priorities, but as long as the weather held, and the machinery didn't break down, and he could bear the pain in his back, there was nothing more important than the hay. Here they were into August already. Periodically he seemed to catch again that faint, revolting stench of death. He must get word to the Mounties.

It was a hot day, almost without a breeze. Each forkful of hay that Jesse and Ethan lifted onto the rack gave off a little trail of chaff and dust that neither fell nor blew away, but seemed to glitter in the sunlight, floating around them as they worked. George drove the team along the windrow, and when he drew abreast of a hay pile, Jesse shouted "Whoa!" George was delighted. He stood on the floor of the hayrack, pressed against its front by the load of hay rising behind him. He was scarcely tall enough to reach his arms over the top board and hold the lines. When the load got as high as they could reach, Ethan climbed on top of it, helped George out of his hole, and then made his way around the outside edge, tromping. The high, fluffy load quickly flattened and spread against the sides of the hay-rack.

Forking up the hay from the ground, Jesse felt the sun of heaven on his shoulders, but low in his back he was suffering the fires of hell. Almost overnight these hills had become a shrine. He was a pilgrim who had crossed the world to get here, and now in the very act of worship, his body betrayed him. The required ritual of the season was haying—but each forkful seemed to press the pain deeper into his back. He was not sure how long he could continue. At last he shouted, "Okay!" and tossed his fork so it sailed like a javelin, dipped, and stuck upright on top of the load. Then he followed, climbing over the rear of the rack, and lay down on the soft, resilient hay. George started the team, and they turned back toward the barn, a half a mile away.

This ride in from the field was the only thing that kept

Jesse going. The gentle bounce and sway of the load seemed to work against his back like a marvelous machine to smooth away the pain. If he could do nothing but ride a load of hay for two weeks steady, he felt as if he'd be as good as new again. But winter didn't wait. Somehow he must keep going till the snow flew; then there would be time to rest his back.

As they approached the barn, George stopped the team. Jesse could not help feeling encouraged. True, they had worked hard for days, but the result of their effort was beginning to show. The hay was stacked under the roof to a height of ten or twelve feet. In fact, they wouldn't be able to fork it much higher. They'd soon have to start a stack out in the field. Maybe next year they could rope the hay off the rack.

Jesse stood up and took the lines from George.

"Can't I try?" George asked.

"I won't even let Ethan try," Jesse said. "We've got to get close, but if there's anything we don't need now, it's a caved-in hayrack or some broken doubletrees." He stood at the front of the load, holding the lines tight. "Giddap!" he called. The team settled into their collars and moved forward. "Hah!" Jesse shouted, leaning back, his arms flexed against the rhythmic pull of the lines as the horses marched close beside the huge logs of the barn. There was a loud hiss when the load came against it, which continued and increased as they moved along. The wagon heaved from the press. "Whoa!" Jesse shouted. The team stopped abruptly. He made a half-hitch with the lines at the top of the hayrack's middle upright, and turned to take his fork.

"Who's that?" Ethan asked.

Jesse looked up the road that led into the yard. A man on horseback was approaching. Even on this hot day he wore a fringed buckskin coat. Horse and saddle and man seemed all of a piece, caked with the same grime and sweat and possessed of a smoldering vitality that rippled through buckskin, horsehide, and the tooled-leather saddle skirts. The man was tall, perhaps fifty years old. Beneath his chin a bush of gray matted hair sprouted from his open shirt. He rode close to the hayrack and stopped, facing Jesse. From the shadow of his broad-brimmed hat, his eyes squinted against the glare of the sun.

"Who are you?" he said.

"Jesse Gifford."

"Where'd you come from?"

"Lone Rock."

"How much she givin' you?"

"What do you mean?"

The man gestured toward the hayrack. He wore gloves that looked as if they had never been off his hands. "Fer puttin' up the hay? I know she ain't got no money to pay ya, so you must be doin' it on shears. How big a shear is she givin' ya?"

"Who are you?" Jesse asked.

"Who am I? What kind of a question is that? This is my hay yer puttin' up." The smell of death came on the wind, stronger than it ever had before.

"You're not Gunderson?" Jesse asked him.

"Who'd ya think I was?" He looked toward the house. "Why ain't she out here? She some kind of lady now—too good to work in the hay?"

"She told me you were dead." He was dead. Jesse saw him clearly, hideously bloated, bursting the seams of his buckskin jacket, caught on a snag in the creek somewhere, tainting the air for miles around. He had lain all day in the cabin while his wife and daughters struggled in the blizzard to dig a grave for him.

Gunderson spoke again. "She told you what?"

"She said you died last winter. She sold the ranch to me."

"She what?" Gunderson laughed. "That sly old bitch. She sold the ranch to you?" He laughed again.

That sly old bitch? Could a simple-minded woman put on an act like that? Mable Gunderson, star of Broadway. Jesse had been completely taken in. But he had the bill of sale, and the title had been in her name. She may have lied about her husband, but the land transfer was legal, whatever Gunderson might say.

"How much did you pay her?" Gunderson asked, still laughing.

"Fifteen hundred dollars."

The man sobered. "Fifteen hundred dollars? Cash?"

"Cash."

He looked at Jesse. "Ho!" he shouted. "Ho! You poor son-of-a-bitch. Ho!" He laughed so hard he doubled over his saddle horn, and for a minute he looked as though he might roll off onto the ground. Then he straightened, looked at the hay barn, and shouted, "Then you ain't got no shear at all. I got my hay put up for free." He laughed again. "Where is she now?"

"I don't know," Jesse said. "She caught the train for somewhere."

Gunderson sobered again. "The bitch! Manitoba! She went back to her goddam brothers." Suddenly he shouted at Jesse, "Get off my ranch."

"You don't have a ranch," Jesse said. "You never had one."

The man sat on his horse, glaring at Jesse. The shadow

[*150*]

of his hat came partway down his face, but where the sun struck them, his cheeks showed a pallor through the brown skin, like milk in an amber glass. "Mister. When we first come out here my wife thought just 'cause she paid for the damn ranch it give her a little say. It took a while, but I learnt her different. I ain't got time to work with you like-a that. Now git down off'n that hay and git up the road. And take them damn cubs with you."

"You're trespassing," Jesse said. "I have a bill of sale to prove it."

The man whooped. "Bill of sale! You're a funny son-of-a-bitch, ain't you? You're like my goddam wife. She had a Duplicate Certificate of Title she told me a thousand times, like it was somethin'. A piece of paper ain't nothin', mister. Up in these hills they ain't nothin' that counts but what's real. I've broke my back workin' this place for seventeen years, mister. That's real. And no goddam piece of paper signed by Jesus H. Christ hisself can take it away from me."

Jesse didn't know what to say.

"Why d'ya think she told you I'se daid?" Gunderson went on. "'Cause she know'd the ranch was mine, that's why. She know'd she had no right to sell it. This whole damn pile of ground is stuck together with my blood, an' the only way any man would touch it is if he figured I'se daid. Yer a stranger here, mister, but you ask any man in forty mile whose ranch this is, and he'll tell you Asa Gunderson's. Just cause I rid away at Christmastime fer a little peace and fresh air ain't the same as if I'se daid. So you suit yourself. You can walk out of here, or you can git carried out, and either way it don't matter a damn to me. You suit yourself."

Jesse didn't want to ignore the man—he seemed

riled enough as it was—but he couldn't think of any way to answer him. He pulled a forkful of hay free from the load and tossed it high into the barn.

"Look out!" Ethan cried.

Jesse spun around just as Gunderson threw his lariat, and his horse turned, dancing, sideways to the hayrack. Jesse saw the small loop flash up at him. He flung up his arms and ducked—too late. The rope whipped around his body, singing through the honda as Gunderson's horse lunged away. Jesse felt himself caught under the arms and yanked over the edge of the load with stupefying force. Instinctively his arms reached out and he grasped the rope that pulled him, while he plunged over the side of the hay load with staggering giant steps. As he crashed against the ground, his leg buckled under him and he was yanked forward onto his stomach, bouncing through the dust behind the galloping horse.

Was this how it ended? Come suicide or Sundown, this was the death they saved for him—dragged at the end of some madman's lariat—storing it till now, just when he'd got a place of his own. He heard Ethan shout behind him. He glimpsed, through the dust, the flashing hooves, and felt the rocks of the barnyard smashing against his sides. Then he closed his eyes and wondered how long it took to drag a man to death.

When he hit the creek he felt the cold water splash in his face, then his body planed onto the water, began to sink and crash against the boulders on the bottom. Suddenly the furious pull on his body stopped, and he sank, floundering, choking, trying to get his twisted leg under him to raise his head above the surface of the water. He felt strong arms around his body lift him, half drag him to the side of the creek, and lay him down on his back among the boulders.

The lariat was taken off over his head. He heard Gunderson laugh, and saw Gunderson's yellow teeth through a blur of water still running down his face.

"You poor son-of-a-bitch," Gunderson said. "Thought I'se goin' to drag you to death, didn't ya? Why, I'm a kindly fellar—I wouldn't do a thing like that. 'Tain't yer fault my old lady lied to ya. But if I ever catch yer face on my land again, I'll strangle ya. Savvy?"

Jesse's vision had cleared a little, and he saw Gunderson get on his horse and ride away. A moment later the faces of his boys appeared above him. "He was going to kill you, wasn't he, Jesse?" Ethan said.

"No. He only wanted to scare us a little." That proved the ranch belonged to Jesse, anyway. If Gunderson had a legal claim, he wouldn't have to use such tactics. Slowly the pain which at first diffused through his whole body began to concentrate in certain areas, like rain water draining into puddles after a heavy shower.

"Boy! He scared me!" Ethan said.

"He's a bad man," George declared.

Jesse tried to twist himself, to relieve the points of contact between his body and the rocks. "You think you were scared!" he said. Suddenly, as he tried to move his leg, the entire weight of pain rushed there, so massive and pervading that he collapsed completely, breathing as though from a long run.

"What's the matter, Jesse?" Ethan said.

"My leg." He couldn't even raise his head to look at it.

The boys looked down toward his right boot. "It's all funny," George said.

"It must be broken," Ethan agreed.

He had been too busy coming off that load of hay to notice what happened when he hit the ground. That was all he needed now, a broken leg. Six weeks in traction, and Gunderson would have his hooks so deep in this ranch that Jesse could never break him loose.

The pain in his leg began to mount. Gingerly he raised enough on his elbows to peek down and see the toe of his boot canted unnaturally to one side. "Have you got your pocketknife?" he asked Ethan.

"Sure," the boy replied.

"Cut off that boot."

"You mean your new boots?"

"Hurry up, 'fore it gets any tighter. And be careful."

The boy was careful, Jesse could tell. Still, he could not help moving the foot a little as he worked, slicing the side of the boot from the top down. When he got to the swollen ankle, the boot was so tight against the skin that it was very difficult to cut, and two or three times it felt to Jesse as though the knife went deep into his swollen flesh. So it was not Gunderson who was bloated and blue, as it should have been, but Jesse himself lying there in a lonely cup of the foothills, a thousand miles from anywhere. What had George said? It was so far away?

"Where'd Gunderson go?" Jesse asked.

Ethan's cut was over the hump of the ankle now, and the pain seemed less severe. "Over the hill, like he was headed for town."

"He didn't say anything?"

"Uh-uh. Just got on his horse and rode off."

Gunderson knew his wife had fifteen hundred dollars —it was possible he might head for Manitoba. On the other hand, he might simply have ridden over the hill and be hiding somewhere watching them, and laughing. Whatever the case, there wasn't much Jesse could do about it right now. He had to get his leg taken care of, and from past experience he knew that could take weeks, maybe months, if it was bad enough. Even if Gunderson went to Manitoba, what would happen to the hay crop? And if, instead, he moved onto the place while Jesse was away, how would they ever get him off? Well, one thing at a time.

"I've got to get to a doctor," Jesse said. "Ethan, you hitch the team onto the democrat, load the box with hay, and bring it over here. George, you go over to the woodpile and see if you can find two straight boards about three feet long. You know how long three feet is? And bring that binder twine that's in the shop."

While the boys were gone, Jesse dragged himself slowly onto a level patch of grass nearby. It was a painful exercise, but he knew that worse was coming. Presently George returned with the boards, and then Ethan came with the democrat. Under Jesse's direction, he placed a board on each side of the injured leg, from the knee down past the heel, and began to wrap it with binder twine. Ethan was so nervous and excited that he tended to wrap it too tight, and twice Jesse had him unwrap it partway and loosen it a bit.

"Now," Jesse said. He wiped his palm across his face, and it was cold as a jug. He hated for the boys to see him like this; on the other hand, he was glad not to be alone. "Fetch a couple of blankets from the house," he said. He had in mind to climb in the democrat while they were gone, so he could moan a little if he had to. Halfway over the wheel, he changed his mind, moaning, and decided to wait for Ethan to help him, but he could no more lower himself than he could pull himself over. He was caught on a pinnacle of pain, where it seemed he might have to hang forever, but the muscles in his arms began to tremble with the weight and stress, and he knew he'd have to do something. With one blinding effort, he hitched his good leg beneath him, heaved with his hands, and pushed upward with all his might. Just as the world went dark, he felt himself roll onto the hay in the box of the democrat.

Consciousness came slowly. He was aware first of the sun in his eyes, then the gentle, rhythmic movement of the hay beneath him. He looked at the sky, almost white in the full blaze of summer. His leg twinged with the movement of the democrat, but it seemed numb now. Then he tried to look about him, and the movement brought the pain rushing back again. He froze, and waited for it to subside, but it took a long time. He heard George's voice from the front of the democrat. "Giddap." Gently tipping his head up, and raising his eyes as high as he could, he made out the crown of the boy's hair, the color of a halo, bouncing across the sky.

"Where's Ethan?" Jesse asked.

"Whoa!" George cried, and pulled on the lines so hard that he sat down almost on top of his father's head. "You all right, Jesse? Gee. I'se scared you was dead."

"You always think I'm dead," Jesse accused him.

"That's what dead people do, isn't it? Just lay there and don't even breathe or anything?"

"Where's Ethan," Jesse repeated.

"He stayed home."

"Stayed home!" Jesse started up, but the pain hit him like a falling hammer, and he lay back again. "That crazy guy will kill him."

"He's guarding the ranch," George said. "I'm s'posed to take you to the hospital."

"Not without Ethan, you're not. We can't leave him back there alone. You saw what that guy did to me."

"Ethan says he can handle him. He says nobody's going to get our ranch now."

[*156*]

"Turn this outfit around, George. 'Fore I trounce you good."

George scrambled to his feet again, and moved out of reach. "Giddap," he said, and they started to move again. "Ethan said you might not like it," he said. "But we got to get you to the doctor. And we got to keep that bad old guy off the ranch. Ethan's doing one, and I'm doing the other."

It took them hours to get there. They tried trotting the team, but it shook the democrat too much, and so they had to travel fifteen miles at a slow walk. The sun was far down in the sky as George drove the team up in the shadow of the hospital, and Jesse was so exhausted that the moment they touched him he blacked out again. This time when he came to, he was in a hospital room with a scaffolding above him, and his right leg stretched upward like a whitewashed log. He remembered the boys, and fumbled at the head of the bed for his buzzer. Presently a nurse appeared.

"Did you see the boy who brought me here?" Jesse asked.

"No. I wasn't on then."

"Could you find out what happened to him? He's only six years old."

"I'll inquire," the nurse replied.

"And something else. Could you call the Mounties for me? Ask them to please send somebody over? Right away?"

The nurse left, and in a few minutes returned. "Nobody saw your boy," she said. "Or at least, they didn't see where he went."

"What time is it?"

"Four o'clock. It'll be getting light soon."

"And he's nowhere around the hospital?"

"No. He had a team and wagon, but they're gone now."

Crazy little George. What was he doing? Did he start

back to the ranch alone—back through the evening foothills into the dark mountains? Lord! What is it you want of me?

The nurse said, "The constable will be right over."

The constable? Oh, yes. The Mountie. "Are they awake at this time of night? Thank you."

When he came, the officer's wide shoulders seemed almost to fill the room. Though he walked in quietly, there was a firm authority in the way his boots clicked on the linoleum floor. "Mr. Gifford?" he said.

"Hello, Officer." Jesse felt the words tumbling up into his mouth faster than he could speak. "Please hurry."

"First you'll have to tell me what you want me to do."

"Save my boys," Jesse said. His face was still cold and damp as he rubbed his palm across it. He couldn't be sure whether the dampness was from tears. "The crazy little beggars. Save my boys."

CHAPTER XXII

AS the light of morning slowly rose in the hospital window, Jesse tried to think how, lying there, he could control the delicate world he had scarcely started to build outside. Napoleon, from banishment, had raised an army. Couldn't Jesse, from his hospital bed, dominate his simple affairs?

The first consideration was the boys. They couldn't stay on the ranch alone, even if there were no Gunderson. But he didn't know a soul in Pincher Creek. If he brought them to town, what could he do with them? Neither was there anyone he could send out to stay with them. In four short years he had managed to end up without a friend in the world.

The second thing was his fight with Gunderson for the ranch.

The third problem was the ranch itself. What would happen to it with nobody there? The cow would go dry. The hay crop would be lost. And if the cattle found a hole in the fence, they might wander back into the mountains and become food for the bears.

Well, he could ask Shirley to come and take the boys, but if she did, he might lose them forever. Without the boys his ranch would be a mockery—he'd about as soon go back to San Soucie.

About midmorning the Mountie returned and stood above him, smiling under the hard, flat brim of his hat. "Those are quite the boys you've got, Mr. Gifford," he said.

"They're all right?" Jesse asked. "You brought them to town?"

"No. I'm afraid this time the Mounties didn't get their man. They're all right. They just don't want to leave the ranch."

"But they've got to leave. There's no telling what Gunderson will do."

"Gunderson won't do anything for a while," the Mountie said. "Yesterday he turned his horse in the community pasture outside town and caught the train for Manitoba. Mr. Burns sold him the ticket and saw him get on the train."

"Thank heaven for that."

"But the boys aren't taking any chances. They won't let anybody on the place."

"What do you mean?"

"Well, I drove out there this morning. But when I got out of the car, they shouted for me to leave."

"They what?"

"I could just see their heads through the window of the house. One had a rifle pointed at me."

"Ethan!" There had been a Winchester carbine hanging on the wall of the Gunderson cabin.

"Is that his name? The one with the rifle did the talking."

"I can't understand it," Jesse said. "I mean, if Gunderson showed up there, maybe so. But why would they stop you?"

"I think they're afraid I might take them with me, and they won't leave till you get home."

"That'll be weeks."

"That's what I told them, but it doesn't matter. They're looking after the ranch."

Jesse turned his face away for a moment. It seemed like a serious offense to threaten a Mountie, and he didn't want the officer to guess that he was proud.

"I could have forced his hand, I guess, and brought him in," the man said. "But to tell you the truth, I liked the boy's spirit. I thought I'd come and discuss it with you."

"It's probably best to leave them alone. Ethan's a good shot—if he's serious, somebody might get hurt. And they can likely take care of themselves as long as Gunderson's away. But I sure don't want to have Ethan trying to outsmart that maniac."

"They should be all right for a week or so," the Mountie said. "In the meantime, I'll try to slip out there once in a while to see how they're doing."

"I'd appreciate it," Jesse said.

For Jesse, the days inched away. He was not in pain, really, but because he had to lie in one position, his discomfort was extreme. The doctor had projected four weeks in traction, followed by several months in a walking cast. That became his goal—the walking cast. With that, at least he could go home. And if Gunderson came around, he could kick him to death with it.

One day the nurse announced visitors, and Ethan and George came in right behind her. Their faces and hands were clean, and their shirt and overalls had apparently just been washed, but not ironed. Ethan was unsure what to do, and he hesitated, but George flung himself up onto the high bed and threw both arms around Jesse's neck.

"Careful, sonny," the nurse said. "You mustn't get up there."

Jesse clasped his arms around the little body. "He's all right," he said. "We'll be all right."

The nurse left them.

Ethan bent over him then, and Jesse extended his embrace to include both of them. For several minutes they just lay there, so close they could feel the thump of each other's hearts. Finally Ethan raised himself up, but George still remained, his arms around his father's neck.

"How's it going out there?" Jesse said.

"Fine. We finished the hay," Ethan replied.

"You what?"

"Well, just what you had cut. We got it all in the barn."

"How did you get it up there? It was so high I could hardly reach."

"We got a rope and an old basket. George fills the basket with hay, and I pull it up into the barn."

Another cricket came and carried off another grain of corn. Ye gods, how had a waster like him fathered boys such as these?

"Of course, it's pretty slow," Ethan continued. "It takes us all day to unload, but we finished today. We had to celebrate, so we decided to come and see you."

George sat up and looked at the strange contraption over the bed. "What's that?" he asked.

"That white thing is my leg," Jesse said. "All the other stuff is just to keep it stretched."

"Stretched?"

"So it'll be the same length when it gets better."

"But if it's stretched, it won't be the same length. It'll be longer."

"When can you come home?" Ethan said.

"Not for three more weeks. When I get my walking cast. Listen, if I can find a place for you fellows to stay, will you come in town? I don't want you out there alone."

"We're all right. Aren't we, George?"

George didn't look at Jesse. "Sure," he said, but his voice was very soft. He nodded his head. "We're all right."

"Besides, somebody has to milk the cow. Tomorrow we're going to start fixing those places in the fence where the cattle might get away."

"Be careful," Jesse said. "Just staple a post in the hole, or something. Don't try to work those wire stretchers."

"We can do it."

"You can snap something too, and wrap a half mile of barbed wire around your neck. We can't take a chance on any more accidents."

"Okay," Ethan said.

"We got to be there when old Gunderson comes back," George said. "We're going to blast his head clean off."

"We're not going to hurt him," Ethan said quickly. "We just won't let him take our ranch away."

"Well, that's something else I want to talk to you about," Jesse said. "The way I figure it, Gunderson is crazy. The only way to treat him is to stay a long ways away. I've

GOLDENROD

got word from the lawyer that our title has been registered, so it doesn't matter how loud he hollers, or how wild he acts, Gunderson doesn't have the ranch. If he's sitting on it when I get out, we'll just take a Mountie home with us and put him off. If you see any sign of Gunderson, get out the back door, and come in here and tell me. You hear?"

"You said yourself he's crazy. He knows the ranch is sold. How do you know he won't steal the cattle, and bust up the machinery, and burn down the house?"

"You're pigheaded, just like your mother, Ethan. You haven't a chance against Gunderson. Look what he did to me."

"He took you by surprise," Ethan said. "But we're ready for him. Aren't we, George?"

George nodded.

"He could kill the both of you!" Jesse exclaimed. "Do you think that lousy ranch means anything to me without you fellows to give me a hand?"

"He won't kill us," Ethan said solemnly.

"All right. Suppose you did get lucky. Suppose you killed him. Is that any better? What good are you hanged or in jail?"

Ethan said, "We'd better get back to the place."

"Do we have to go already?" George cried.

"Ethan," Jesse said. "You've got to listen to me."

"I have to take care of the ranch," the boy replied.

George climbed up and gave Jesse a squeeze good-bye, but Ethan stood back, away from him.

"Don't go yet," Jesse said. "Let's talk awhile."

"No. We'd better go," Ethan said. "I don't like to be away too long." At the door, he paused and looked back. "I don't know if we'll get in to see you again, Jesse. Gunderson might get back any time now. We can't leave the place."

[163]

"Good-bye, Daddy," George said. And the boys were gone.

Gunderson might get back any time now. That was true. And when he did get back, what would happen? If Jesse went home, and rigged himself a bed with a rope and a stone pulling on his foot, couldn't he heal up just as well as here? But suppose he did. And suppose Gunderson came. What a laugh that would be! There was only one thing to do, and that was get the boys off the ranch. And he could think of only one way to do that. He asked the nurse to phone Shirley for him and see if she would come.

CHAPTER XXIII

HE had been dozing when she walked in, and she approached the bed so quietly that he didn't know she was there until he heard the chair scrape. He opened his eyes just as she sat down. At first it seemed like a dream.

"Hello," she said.

"Thanks for coming."

"What have you been up to?"

"Oh, just a small case of a broken leg. I got yanked off a haystack by a dead man, if you can believe that."

"You sound like you're still coming out of the ether," she said. "Where are the boys?"

"That's why I wanted you to come." As briefly as he could, he told her the story.

"So you really bought a ranch," she said when he was through.

"Oh, it's not much. Just prairie wool and dandelion. But it's good enough for us. We can live on it."

"What do you want me to do?"

"The boys are sitting out there waiting for Gunderson to show up. Before he comes, I want them off the place, and you're the only person I know that can walk in there and talk to them."

She smiled. "You want me to get shot at?"

"They won't shoot at you, and you know it."

"Come on. Don't be so serious."

"But this is serious business. Ethan won't want to leave. If you have to hogtie him, do it."

"You forget," she said. "He's as big as I am now."

"You'll know what to do."

"How do I get to the place?"

"It's only fifteen miles. You have a car? You can be there in half an hour."

When he had given her directions, she rose and walked out of the room. He could see her body beneath the red cotton dress, curved and soft as it had always been.

Two days went by. Every moment Jesse expected to see them come through the door. First he wondered what took them so long. Then he began to worry for fear Gunderson had returned and there'd been trouble. Finally he realized that she must have taken the boys and returned directly to Keno's. They hadn't even stopped to see him.

But on the second afternoon Shirley and George came walking in, hand in hand, laughing together. George climbed up and hugged his father. Shirley let her cool palm rest on his arm for just a moment. Her lips were smiling. "How are you?" she asked. "Did you think we were never coming? We had work to do, didn't we, George?"

"We sure did. We washed the windows. Mama scrubbed on the outside and I scrubbed on the inside, and we pulled faces at each other."

"I've never seen such a place," Shirley said. "Well, you know some of the places we've moved into. They were nothing. No—thing. But we got a good start. We found the house really has a board floor under all that dirt. We washed all the bedding, and it's hanging on the line right now. Ethan made three trips to the junk pile with the wheelbarrow full of stuff we threw away."

"Where is Ethan?"

"He wouldn't come. He had to stay and guard the ranch."

"I told you to get him off that place."

"Jesse, I tried. But he's just as stubborn as you are. He gets his mind made up, there's nothing anybody can do."

"And you left him out there all alone?"

"You did want to know what was happening, didn't you?"

"Of course I did . . ."

"Well, what else could I do?"

"Knock him over the head. Get him drunk. Kidnap him. I don't care what you do. But get him away from there."

"No," she said coolly, and sat down in the chair. "I've decided what to do. You'll be in here another couple of weeks. Since the boys won't come with me, I'll stay with them for that long."

"You're as bad as Ethan. Do you think Gunderson would hesitate to break your neck?"

"I don't know. But I think Ethan is right. It's important to stay on the place. What do they say—possession is nine tenths of the law?"

"Nine points, I think."

"Nine points. Nine tenths. Whatever it is. You've paid for the place, and I don't think anybody should walk in and take over just because it's unoccupied. Especially after we've just cleaned it up."

"And stacked the hay," George said.

"And fixed the fence," Shirley added.

Jesse groaned. "So here I have you come down to help, and all you do is join the enemy."

"We're not the enemy," Shirley said. "Are we, George?"

"No. We're your friends."

"What about Keno?" Jesse asked.

"I'll phone him and tell him not to expect me for a week or two."

"Is he going to like that?"

"Probably not."

"But I just can't let you do it," Jesse said. "It's too risky.

"Oh? And how are you going to stop us?" She reached into her handbag. "We brought the crib board," she said. She smoothed a place for the board on the side of the bed and handed the deck to him to shuffle. "Come on. We haven't payed crib for a long time." Her slender fingers pressed the pegs into place. Jesse began to shuffle the cards. To him, it seemed that perhaps in a previous life he might have played cribbage with Shirley.

After that, Shirley and George came to see him every afternoon with reports on progress at the ranch. The house was clean. Their clothes were mended. The fence was fixed. The hens were laying more eggs. One of the mares had a new colt. Jesse almost began to wish that his time in the hospital would be extended. He lived quite happily from one afternoon to the next, and somehow even the dark shadow of Gunderson began to grow hazy in his mind.

Then one day they were late. His first thought was Gunderson. He'd had time to go to Manitoba and get that money from his wife, and now he was back to claim the ranch as well. Nothing belonged to him, yet he would have it all. Jesse pictured his wife and boys pitted against Gunderson. How could he have been so foolish? Why had he let the situation continue? Surely he could have done something, even if he'd had the three of them put in jail. They were his responsibility, and once more he had failed them. This time, though, he might never have another chance.

Toward evening Shirley and George came in. They were walking slowly, but they smiled.

"Did Gunderson come back?" Jesse asked.

"Quit worrying about Gunderson," Shirley replied. "If he comes, we'll just give him a piece of pie full of broken glass."

"That guy couldn't tell the difference," Jesse said. "He'd think it was peanuts."

"Forget about Gunderson. We've had a big day."

"We went to J. T. Jones'," George said.

"We brought some of your things," Shirley said. "The dishes and shotgun and bedding. And your trophy saddle. It's beautiful."

Jesse nodded.

"You'll have to make another trip sometime, of course. Buster's still waiting there in the pasture."

"I thought maybe the Indians would have been over and stolen everything by now."

Shirley shrugged. "No sign of any burglars. Of course, I don't know what you had." Then she added, "The little photograph was still on the table."

"Yes," he said. "I kept it for the boys. So they wouldn't forget you."

Why did he say things like that? He didn't keep it for the boys. He kept it by his bed for him—to torture him every night before he went to sleep, and every morning when he woke up, because even the misery of remembering was better than the limbo he floated in when he tried to pretend she didn't exist.

GOLDENROD

"I'm tired," she said. "It was cold today. No sun, and a cold wind blowing. I guess our summer is over."

"And I had to spend it in here," Jesse said.

"You didn't do too badly for one season. You won the championship, and you got your ranch."

"I guess I did get kind of lucky."

"Do you know when you'll be able to come home?"

She was anxious to get back to Keno. "About a week, I guess."

"Maybe I could stay an extra day or two, and help you get settled."

"That would be great, if you could," he said. "I'll probably be pretty awkward when they turn me loose."

"Of course, if you don't think it would be right . . . I mean, proper . . ." She was almost blushing.

Look who was talking about proper! She was still his wife, wasn't she? It would be a lot more proper than for her to go back to Keno. "You'll be safe," he said. "I couldn't catch Hungry Dog's grandmother with this fence post of a leg."

"What if I didn't run?" Shirley asked.

He had begun to open his mouth, with something in mind to say, but at her words it seemed his senses dissolved, or were burned in the sudden rush of his desire. All he wanted to do was put his arms around her, to heal the wound that had lain open for so long. He couldn't speak, for fear he'd reveal his confusion. She sat, not speaking either, while the color rose in her cheeks. "We'd better go," she said. For a moment she rested her hand on his. "Hurry home."

CHAPTER XXIV

THE next day they didn't come at all. From early morning Jesse had begun to watch for them. Over and over in his mind, he brought back the words she'd spoken yesterday. Had she meant something more than the words themselves said? If she was trying to tell him something, why didn't she just come out and say it? Surely they knew each other well enough that they didn't have to play games.

Then, when the day passed and she didn't come at all, he felt that she'd been leading him on—deliberately playing with him. In reality she was just waiting to get back to Keno.

Darkness came. Slowly the activity of the hospital subsided. The nurse prepared him for sleep and turned out his light, but the corridor still cast some of its brightness into the room. The building seemed to hum on one low, reassuring note, and now in the quiet of the night he could hear a woman far down the hall cry out repeatedly in broken English, "My baby! I want my baby!"

He didn't feel like sleeping. He didn't even want to sleep. Still, in time, he began to drowse.

He became aware of someone near him, and opened his eyes. There was a shadowy figure crouched on the side of his bed away from the door. It spoke in a whisper: "Jesse."

"Ethan. What are you doing here?"

"Shh. I sneaked in."

"What's the matter? What happened? Did Gunderson come?"

[*170*]

"No. Keno."

"Keno?"

"He came to take Mama. He says she's going back with him."

"What does she say?"

"She says she won't leave George and me alone. So he says all right. They'll take us too."

"So?"

"That's when I got out. I'm not going to live with that guy."

"Did he chase you?"

"I ran out the door, and George started after me, but he grabbed George and held him. So I got on a horse and headed up in the hills. I watched to see what would happen. I was afraid he'd just take Mama and George and go. But then I thought he'd have to come back for his other car, and when he did, maybe you'd be home and we could split his skull."

"Don't talk that way."

"If it wasn't for him, everything would be all right now. Why did Mama ever go with him anyway?"

"I don't know."

"Well. Then after a while he got out the other horse and came looking for me. I kept ahead of him all right, but I was scared, Jesse. I didn't know what to do. I decided the best thing was to come and talk to you. But he had me cut off from the road, so I had to go 'way back through the hills."

"Shirley's still home?"

"Far as I know. She and George are at the house, and Keno's beating the bushes for me."

It was one thing for a man to take your wife away from you, if she went of her own accord. It seemed to Jesse like something else to kidnap your whole family. "Can you tell if Shirley wants to go or stay?" Jesse said.

"She wants to stay."

"Did she say so?"

"Not exactly, I guess. But I can tell. Jesse, you don't know how much fun we've had since she came. It's just like old times." Then he added, "'Cept we needed you, of course."

"Well, I'm coming home with you right now."

Ethan looked at the overhead bars, and ropes and weights. "You can't," he said. "Not till they take this stuff off you."

"We've got to be quiet," Jesse said. "We can't turn on the light and we can't shut the door. So we've got to be careful, and quiet. Now first thing to do is untie that rope from the hook in my cast. Be sure you've got hold of the weight. If we drop one of those, we might as well blow a bugle to tell them we're going."

"D'you think we ought to?"

"We're doing it, aren't we? Now hurry up."

Ethan had a firm hold on the weight when the end of the rope slipped free, but the leg in the cast fell like a log to the bed. At first Jesse felt as though he could not move it. He raised himself, trying to sit on the edge of the bed. "Look in that closet," he said. "See if my clothes are there."

Ethan groped inside the little cupboard. "Just a shirt and some overalls," he said. "And your boots. It's cold tonight. You can't go without a coat."

Jesse motioned for the boy to bring the clothes. He put the shirt on over his hospital gown. "Where's your pocket-knife?" he asked. He took it and slit the outside seam on the right side of his overalls from top to bottom. Then he pulled them on over his good leg, with the belt holding them

together at the top and the right leg flapping free. The cast
came up to his knee. Above that his thigh was partly bare.
He slipped on his left sock and boot. Then he slid off the
bed and balanced on one foot. The room seemed to turn
and slant a bit. He caught Ethan's shoulder with his hand.

"How do you feel?" the boy asked.

"Like I haven't been out of bed for three weeks," he
said. "I'm dizzy."

"How's the leg?"

"It's okay. I wish I had a crutch."

"I wish you had a sheepskin coat."

"How did you get in here without getting caught?"

"I just watched at the door, and when nobody was
around, I sneaked in."

Jesse hopped carefully over to the window. It slid up
easily, and the cold wind rushed in around him. "Let's go
this way," he said. "You first."

Ethan put both legs through the window, and hanging
on to the sill with his hands, let himself down. When he had
fully extended his arms, he said, "How far is it?"

Jesse was bending above him. "It's not far," he said.
"You can drop."

Ethan let go. There was a slight *swish* as his coat sleeves
slipped over the window sill, then a *chuck* when his boots
struck the ground. He looked up at Jesse. "Okay," he said.
"Come on."

First Jesse put the leg with the cast out the window.
Luckily they were at the rear of the hospital, away from the
street, or somebody would spot them sure. The wind blew
against his toes and his exposed thigh, and fluttered his
shirt. He put his other leg through the window, paused a
moment sitting on the sill, let himself slip downward as he
turned over. His hip joint ached with the sudden weight of

the cast. He lowered himself, hesitated, dropped, trying to hold the cast up, staggered when he landed, and tipped dizzily against the side of the building. Slowly he rolled on his good leg until he was facing outward.

"Where's your horse?" Jesse said.

"Just around the corner." Ethan took Jesse's right arm across his shoulder. "Come on. I'll help you."

But the ground had not quit reeling, and Jesse still leaned with his shoulders against the wall. "Can you bring him here?"

"Sure. If they don't see us."

"They can't stop me now."

"You should have brought a blanket. You're going to freeze to death."

"Bring the horse."

While Ethan was gone, Jesse leaned against the wall. He felt as if he had no substance—as if the cold wind were blowing right through him, shaking his bones as it would the branches of a tree in winter. Slowly, though, the ground came up firmly beneath his good foot and the building quit shifting behind his shoulders. Now the only thing that moved was the wind, slipping its cold fingers over his half-naked body. When the horse came he took the saddle horn in both hands, hesitated, lifted his left foot in one swift motion to the stirrup, raised himself, and with the help of his hand, crossed his broken leg over the cantle till it dropped like a stone on the other side of the horse. He kicked his good foot free of the stirrup, put his hand down for Ethan, and the boy swung up behind him. The horse turned nervously, spooked by the white leg, until Jesse slackened the reins, and he galloped onto the road, then turned south out of town.

They couldn't see any stars above them. The wind had

almost stopped. Now the night seemed sealed in an unearthly stillness. The only sound was the soft click of the horse's hooves on the road, and the creak of the saddle. Random flakes of snow began to drift down out of the black sky.

"Snow," Jesse said. "And not yet September." He could feel the flakes on his thigh now, coming faster—feel them land and melt in overlapping rings of cold. "I hate winter," he said. "Especially when it comes early. It seems as if we never had summer—nothing but cold winds howling from one December to the next."

CHAPTER XXV

THE sound of the horse's hooves became muffled by the falling snow. Jesse and Ethan moved silently through the myriad flakes that settled from a blacker and blacker sky. Jesse's hands gripped the pommel in front of him. Ordinarily his saddle was like a second home—he could sleep in it if he had to, like a bird in a tree. But tonight he felt that without Ethan's arms around him, he would roll off onto the ground, and soon be covered by the snow—a small hump in the flat whiteness that spread like a carpet on the floor of the night.

When they started over the hill above the ranch buildings, Jesse was reminded of another ride leading down into darkness—the evening they first arrived at J. T. Jones'. Less than three months ago that had been, yet it seemed that years had passed. He had learned, on that occasion, to hope for nothing. How grim life's lessons are, he thought, and how easily forgotten.

At the bottom of the hill they rode past the barn, low and horizontally striped by the snow that lay on the upper curves of the logs.

The boy spoke at last. "What are you going to do, Jesse?"

"I don't know."

They could see the light in the cabin window, where white flakes turned black as they crossed in front of it. A truck and car sat near by—Keno's light delivery and the Buick that Shirley had brought when she came. The truck sat high and straight, like a stiff-necked man in a white cap, but the Buick seemed to crouch beneath its mounds of snow, its fenders curled like paws, ready to leap forward.

The horse stopped. Ethan slid to the ground. When Jesse followed him, the weight of the cast pulled him down with a rush that almost broke his hands away from the saddle horn. He clung on, and managed to keep his good foot under him while he waited for his strength and steadiness to return.

"Come on," Ethan said.

Jesse put his right arm over the boy's shoulder, and partly hopping, partly hobbling on his cast, he covered the distance to the house and leaned against the wall. Ethan opened the door.

Shirley and George, sitting at the kitchen table, looked around.

"Jesse!" Shirley rose from her chair. "Jesse, what are you doing . . . ?"

George ran to him. "Jesse. You're home at last."

The three of them clustered around him and helped him into the bedroom, getting in the way and stumbling over each other like three men moving a single kitchen chair.

[*176*]

"What did you do?" Shirley scolded. "Break out of the hospital?" She threw back the bed covers.

Jesse sat heavily on the side of the bed.

"Just a minute," Shirley said as he moved to lie down. "Let's take off those wet things. You boys wait in the kitchen, will you?"

Reluctantly they backed out of the room. Shirley brought the lamp from the kitchen and set it on a shelf against the wall. She closed the bedroom door.

"Hey," Ethan called. "It's dark out here."

"I'll only be a few minutes." She started to unbutton Jesse's shirt.

Jesse fumbled at the buttons, but his fingers were too cold to do any good. "Where's Keno?" he asked.

"Maybe he's lost. He took a horse and went to look for Ethan. When I heard you come, I thought it was him. I was scared, Jesse. I didn't know what to do."

She pulled off the shirt. Then, while he sat on the bed, she reached her arms around his neck to untie the top string of his hospital gown. He put his hands on her waist, and when he felt its slender softness, and the firm swell of her hips, a chain of recollection was begun in him, as if with whole body, he remembered all of hers. So deep inside his loins it seemed to touch the very quick of him, a seed put down its root.

"Shirley."

She drew back. The hospital gown came off over his arms. She unbuckled his belt and began to slide his overalls down. "You'll have to raise up," she said.

"The boot, first."

"Oh, yes." She laughed, and pulled off his left boot and the sock.

He lifted himself, slipped his trousers down, and she

[177]

pulled them off over his legs. As he rolled into bed, she spread the blankets over him. He couldn't stop shivering. She folded the covers back to his waist, and began to rub his body with a towel, drying and warming it, finally caressing it with the gentle pressure of her hands through the towel. She reached under the blanket and rubbed his stomach, and his legs, and casually brushed his genitals.

His palms were still electric from the touch of her, and the tree that grew out of his heated loins could not endure the rough towel on its tender bark.

"Shirley." He reached for her again. "Stay home. Come back to us."

She had moved to arrange the covers around his feet. "You don't want me back," she said.

"It's all Ethan talks about. You coming back."

"Yes. Ethan would take me back. Ethan and George."

"I'll take you back."

She looked down at him, her face solemn.

"Remember how it used to be, when the boys were little?" he asked.

She shook her head, and the dark hair swung against her neck. "Keno will never let me stay."

"Well, I won't let you go."

They heard hoofbeats approach through the snow, and stop abruptly just outside. There was the ring of a bridle bit, and a moment later the door swung open. "Where's the light?" Keno's voice shouted as he came inside. "Has everybody in here gone to bed?"

Shirley opened the bedroom door.

"Oh, there you are. Did the kid get back? His horse is ..." He must have seen the boys then, by the lamplight from the bedroom. "Well, thank the Lord. Now we can go."

"There's been a change of plan," Shirley said.

Keno came to the bedroom door and looked in, his coat still on, his hat pushed back on his forehead. "Well, damn me."

"I'll be staying awhile, to take care of Jesse."

"Like hell you will. You and me are goin' home."

"She's already home," Jesse told him.

"Bushwah! This ragtag and haywire outfit!" Keno laughed.

"I can't leave Jesse alone."

"He won't be alone. This just means we won't have to take those damn kids with us now."

"They're my children."

"Well, they're not mine. Come on. It's snowing harder all the time. We've got to go."

"Go ahead."

Keno was tall, standing in the doorway. He looked the same as he always had—dark, smiling, erect. The champ. But as Shirley spoke, he turned, and for a second it was as if a beacon had crossed him, revealing a heavy gray face with dull eyes that stared back at the nonexistent light. And Jesse realized that Keno was vulnerable. It had come too easily for him—the championship, the money, the ranch, the girl. He'd gotten them all. Then he'd rested. For years now he'd rested, and he was soft. Not Jesse. Jesse never had a chance to rest. His struggle may have been feeble and degrading, but it had demanded all the strength he had. Now he was hard as a horn.

But Keno's eyes were bright and powerful again. "Stay, then," he said. "Stay your whole damn life, for all I care. I'm going home."

He left the bedroom; they heard his boots cross the kitchen floor, the sound of a chair overturning, and then the door slam shut behind him.

[*179*]

"He's gone," Ethan said.

The boys ran to the bedroom window and pressed their faces to it between hands cupped against the lamplight. "He's putting his chains on."

"He'll need them to get up the hill," Jesse said.

They waited for the sound of the truck starting, but the night remained silent. Presently they heard footsteps on the porch again.

Keno came in and stamped the snow off his boots. "First time I ever see snow in August," he called. They heard him fumbling in the dark kitchen cupboard, and then he appeared at the bedroom door, half a bottle of whiskey in one hand and three glasses threaded onto the fingers of the other. "Bein' as how old Jesse just got out of the hospital, I thought we should have a little drink before we go."

No one answered him.

Keno sat down on the chair at the foot of the bed and pulled the cork out of the bottle with his teeth. "Just damn lucky I had this in the truck. I almost forgot about it." He set the three glasses on the floor and poured a slosh of whiskey in each of them. Shirley handed one to Jesse, and he raised himself on his elbow.

Keno lifted his arm. "Well, Jesse," he said. "This'll put spine in your busted leg." He tipped up his glass.

Jesse sipped his drink. The liquor made a warm path down his throat into the icy center of his body, and from that path a radiance spread through him. He felt his rigid muscles begin to melt. He sipped again.

Ethan and George stood in the bedroom door, watching them.

Keno sat with the bottle in one hand and his glass in the other. His eyes were on Jesse. The look of the champ. Jesse had beat him out at the stampede, and still Keno wore the look of the champ. What kind of sense did that make?

Keno poured himself another drink. "Damn you, Jesse. I got to admit it. You're a bronc-bustin' son-of-a-bitch." He took a gulp from his glass. "You got an eye for women, too. You take Shirl there. Damn me, she is some woman, for all she cries a lot. And when she ain't cryin' . . . Or sometimes even when she is. I just can't leave go of her, Jesse, that's a fact."

Jesse threw back the covers and sat up on the edge of the bed. "Get out of here, Keno."

Keno drained his glass. "I see you're free enough to drink my whiskey, Jesse. But never mind, we're going. Come on, Shirl." He picked up Shirley's suitcase from where it stood in the corner and flung it open on the floor. He took her clothes from the hangers on the wall and tossed them in, and then her shoes from under the bed. He snapped the suitcase shut. "Come on." He threw her coat at her. "Sooner or later you're goin' to need old Keno, and you know it."

Shirley stood up. She looked down at Jesse, where he sat on the bed. He could see her eyes glistening. "Oh, Jesse."

Keno swung his arm full across her face, so hard that she fell against the foot of the bed.

There was something unreal about it. For a moment Jesse felt as though he were watching a silent film. There should have been a scream at least, and sobs, and there was nothing. And then there came to Jesse the sudden weight of understanding. In the uneven war between Shirley and Keno, silence had become her defense. How she must have fought until she learned it. He longed to restore what Keno had destroyed in her, and he realized that he was not afraid of Keno any more.

Though he sat naked and disarmed, his right leg was still gauntleted in hard white armor. He concentrated all his strength in that one frail weapon, and raised it into Keno's groin. It didn't have the force he wanted, and his aim was slightly off; still, Keno bent forward with a yelp, and Jesse stood up, head first into Keno's solar plexus. Keno went down, writhing. On his feet now, Jesse swung that massive leg against the side of Keno's head. He was drawing it back for another swing when Keno, with a desperate sweep of his arm, knocked Jesse's good leg out from under him. He fell on his back. The corners of the room rocked. He struggled to roll or sit up, but he felt as if he were paralyzed.

Keno's dark countenance rose above him, and he saw Keno's fist coming, slowly at first like a train seen from a distance, then faster, until, with a rush and a roar, it slammed against his face. He struck back, but perhaps he had spent all his strength on that first kick. His punches had no impact. Another fist landed on his own face, and another; solid, methodical, workmanlike blows that seemed to be hammering him down beneath the threshold of consciousness.

A terrible sound erupted in the room—a roar that rushed outward against the walls and rebounded again and again. Keno half rose and turned, his face suddenly gray and the look of death on it, as if he could feel the lead already in his body, like flying worms. But splinters flew in the log wall above them, and Jesse knew the shot was high. The air was heavy with the smell of powder. Ethan still held the shotgun, but the recoil had flung him back against the wall opposite the bedroom floor. He pumped the action. The bright red casing of the spent shell spun out against the wall, fell, and rolled with a hollow sound in a semicircle until it stopped against Keno's foot.

"Next time I'll aim lower," Ethan said.

Jesse rolled onto his stomach, rose on his hands and knees, and climbed unsteadily up to sit on the bed. His fumbling hands pulled a blanket around his body. When he shook his head, it seemed to ring like a bell. How could he concentrate with a church tower sitting on his shoulders?

"Give me the gun, Ethan."

"Let me shoot him, Jesse. If you do it, they'll hang you."

"Do as I say."

Ethan edged into the room, always careful that Keno was able to look straight down into the shiny black insides of the shotgun.

Keno still held the crouched position he had taken when he heard the shot. Only his head moved, slowly turning so his eyes could follow the muzzle of the shotgun, like a bird watching a snake.

Jesse took the gun.

As the barrel stopped moving, Keno raised his eyes from it and rested them on Jesse. Drops of sweat ran down the wet, gleaming sides of Keno's face. His voice seemed to drag over his throat like a chain.

"They'll hang you, Jesse."

Jesse glanced toward Shirley, standing so straight she seemed to be tipping backward. She turned her head quickly to the side, and back again. Her face was flushed, and her eyes bright, as though she were ashamed of something. His nakedness?

Keno started to speak again, but in the end he only licked his lips and continued to stare.

They'll hang you, Jesse.

Jesse almost smiled. He wasn't going to hang. And he wasn't going to wonder who was champ any more, either.

What a difference it made to have a loaded shotgun in his hands. Why, he could make old Keno crawl out of there on his knees if he wanted to.

He had the words already in his mouth: "Get down on your knees, Keno." But before he could speak them, bile came up in his throat, and the words were drowned. He realized that he, too, was ashamed.

Jesse drew the stock of the shotgun back tight against his shoulder. With a rapid motion he pumped the action twice. Two shells flipped out onto the floor, still carrying their lead. They landed heavily, and stayed.

Jesse lay the shotgun on the bed beside him. "Keno's going home," he said to Shirley. "Do you want to go with him, or stay with us?"

"Stay with us!" George cried.

"No!" Jesse said. "We're not telling you what to do. George wants you to stay, and Ethan wants you to stay." He could not believe how coolly he spoke. "I want you to stay, if that's what you want."

Shirley took a step toward him.

"Whatever you decide is all right with Keno. Isn't it, Keno?"

Keno didn't reply. He stood as tall and square as ever, but he seemed to have been drained of substance, as if, should they open the door, the wind would blow him against the cabin wall.

"Ethan," Jesse said. "Will you and George show Mr. Ingram where that pile of rocks is down by the barn? He'll need some weight in his truck before he can get up the hill."

"Sure, Jesse." The boys went through the door. "Let's go, Mr. Ingram."

Keno looked at Shirley. "You coming?"

"You'll have to hurry," she told him. "The snow's getting deeper all the time."

"You can come if you want to. You heard what he said."
He picked up the whiskey bottle from the floor. "Good
Lord. You don't really want to stay!"

Shirley sat down beside Jesse.

Keno stared at her. "What in hell has happened?" His
face changed from anger to pride to contempt, as if he were
an actor trying on masks, but uncertain what part he ought
to play. "My God! I only came down here out of the good-
ness of my heart, to get you away from this mess. And here
you are, feelin' so sorry for old Jellybones you don't know
whether to swallow or spit. Well, it don't matter a damn to
me. Anything you got is waitin' on every street corner." He
tipped his head back and drained the bottle. "So when you
get sick of this godforsaken hole, don't call for Keno. I'll be
busy."

When he turned, his maneuver seemed to take up half
the room. The empty bottle still in his hand, he walked
through the door, across the kitchen, and outside. They
heard the truck door slam, the engine start with a roar, and
saw its headlights scan the room as it circled toward the
barn. The heavy thump of chains moved quickly away into
the storm.

Shirley sat so still that she might have been carved from
wood. Then a tear slipped down over the curve of her
cheek. "Oh, Jesse. I've been such a fool."

"Maybe not. Would you rather we were back at San
Soucie's?"

"No."

Neither would he, Jesse thought. Was it possible that
anything good could come from so much pain? "Suppose
we could start over."

"Suppose," she mused. "If supposes were roses, I'd
make a bouquet. If wishes were fishes, I'd catch some today." She almost smiled. "You used to wish for a ranch."

The path of the tear down her cheek was still visible, like the scar of an ancient wound. He wiped it away with his finger. "Tonight I wish for you."

"Just because you already have your ranch."

She was teasing him. He tried to think of something to say, but his mind was in a kind of jubilant confusion, and his throat so choked with wonder that for a moment he couldn't have spoken anyway.

Abruptly she sobbed and turned her head toward his shoulder. "I don't know how you could want me now."

Because my arms are shaped to you, like the twisted root of a tree when the stone it grew around has washed away. "I love you, Shirl. I've never stopped loving you."

He felt her hand against his body, drawing him to her. "Jesse."

She raised her face, and he could see in her eyes the reflection of the lamp, as soft and bronze as swaying fields of goldenrod.